We Are the Champions

A Cobalt City Universe Story

Erik Scott de Bie

Other Cobalt City Universe Stories

By Nathan Crowder
Greetings From Buena Rosa (2006, Timid Pirate Publishing)
Ride Like the Devil (2007, Timid Pirate Publishing; reprinted 2018, DefCon One Publishing)
Chanson Noir: Protectorate Vol. 1 (2009, Timid Pirate Publishing)
Cobalt City Blues: Protectorate Vol. 2 (2010, Timid Pirate Publishing)
Cobalt City: Los Muertos (2014)
Cobalt City: Ties that Bind (2015; reprinted 2018, DefCon One Publishing)
Cobalt City: Resistance (2018)
The Calling: Red Stag & the Wild Hunt Vol. 1 (2020)

By Amanda Cherry
Rites and Desires (2018, Def Con One Publishing)

By Erik Scott de Bie
Eye for an Eye (originally published as a part of Cobalt City Double Feature, 2012, Timid Pirate Publishing; reprinted 2018, DefCon One Publishing)

By Amanda Cherry and Erik Scott de Bie
Femmes Fatale (2022, DefCon One Publishing)

By Dawn Vogel
Sparx and Arrows (2016, DefCon One Publishing)
Coast to Coast Stars (2020, DefCon One Publishing)
Sure Shot in Las Capas: The Case of the Absent Star (2021, DefCon One Publishing)
Avatar of Freya (2022, DefCon One Publishing)

By Jeremy Zimmerman
Kensei (originally published as a part of Cobalt City Rookies, 2012, Timid Pirate Publishing; reprinted 2014, DefCon One Publishing)
The Love of Danger (2015, DefCon One Publishing)
The Devil, You Say (2015, DefCon One Publishing)
Snowflake War Journal (2016, DefCon One Publishing)
Kensei Tales: Offensive Driving (2016, DefCon One Publishing)
Kensei Tales: It's the Great Yule Cat, Jamie Hattori (2016, DefCon One Publishing)
Kensei Tales: Live and In Concert (2017, DefCon One Publishing)
Kensei Tales: Unorthodoxy (2017, Def Con One Publishing)

Cobalt City Anthologies
Cobalt City Christmas (2009, Timid Pirate Publishing)
Cobalt City Timeslip (2010, Timid Pirate Publishing)
Cobalt City Dark Carnival (2011, Timid Pirate Publishing)
Cobalt City Double Feature (2012, Timid Pirate Publishing, featuring Eye for an Eye by Erik Scott de Bie and The Place Between by Minerva Zimmerman)
Cobalt City Rookies (2012, Timid Pirate Publishing, featuring Tatterdemalion by Nikki Burns, Wrecker of Engines by Rosemary Jones, and Kensei by Jeremy Zimmerman)

Cobalt City Christmas: Christmas Harder (2016)
Cobalt City Dragonstorm (2021)

CONTENTS

Dedication   Pg 1

Acknowledgements   Pg 3

Chapter 1   Pg 5

Chapter 2   Pg 13

Chapter 3   Pg 29

Chapter 4   Pg 39

Chapter 5   Pg 55

Chapter 6   Pg 67

Chapter 7   Pg 81

Chapter 8   Pg 93

Chapter 9   Pg 113

About the Author   Pg 117

For Justice, or Something!

ACKNOWLEDGEMENTS

This book flows directly out of a Cypher campaign run by Nathan Crowder, founder and chief creative of Cobalt City, that introduced a new generation of superheroes to Cobalt City. Started up in 2016, the game dealt with real-life issues of rising fascism in addition to the expected teen superhero fare. This story happens within canon of that game, as I took over for Nate and ran a game that took place during Spring Break, but as Yumi was gone, I needed a good explanation of what she was up to—Nationals!

Special thanks go to the other members of the JOS crew: Dawn Vogel, Jeremy Zimmerman, Rosemary Jones, and James Do Hung Lee. They were instrumental in the creation and development of Yumi Kujikawa, who started out as a borderline shonen heroine and became so much more. Thanks also go to Kelsey Dawn Scott, Kai Ford, Alexandra Pitchford, and Amanda Ratchford Cherry, all of whom played important roles in the development of this story and characterization. Much love to Lori Krell for her remarkable cover and excellent artwork in general. And, of course, a special thank you to Dawn and Jeremy at DefCon One Publishing for making this fun thing I wrote turn into something publishable!

And thanks to my Kickstarter backers! Your patronage has brought this story to life.

CHAPTER 1

Cobalt City, March 2018

Something crackles in the bushes just off the path where the two women are strolling back in the vague direction of the U. Neither of them seems to hear.

"There is great bar I think you like," one of them is saying, her accented words a little slurred with drink. "The Little Dutchgirl. You really like it."

"Um," Lisa Yamamoto says. "Why's it called that?"

"You don't know story?" Her companion—a junior, Svanka, Svetlana, something like that?—replies with a knowing smile and her smooth Russian accent. She stretches in that languid, graceful way ballet dancers and yoga instructors can, and brushes a lock of Lisa's rainbow-dyed hair over her ear. "I won't spoil surprise. You love it."

Lisa has really come out of her shell this past year. She started her freshman year at Cobalt City U as a sheltered, retiring, shy lily of a girl. Now, as a sophomore, she's loosened up and allowed herself to have a little fun. She's still shy and geeky, of course—still really into manga and Magical Girl anime, and she blushes at the tiniest little joke—but she isn't quite as timid as before. She doesn't, after all, faint when a hot Russian girl with an undercut asks her to a lesbian bar. That's progress.

The man in the bushes crouches lower, grinning lewdly. He snaps a few pictures with his smartphone. Slowly, keeping his gaze on the girls, he teases his belt out of its buckle.

"Hey."

His body goes taut. There are few things quite as surprising as someone just talking conversationally to you when you think you're safely hidden.

He looks around, and there she is: clad in a leather and spandex outfit that's half-biker, half-kendo uniform, all badass, with two long scarves that trail from her neck like bits of cape. If homeboy played JRPGs, which he definitely doesn't, he'd probably recognize the homage to a popular PS4 game released pretty recently. But oh well. Her mask is a full-on kendo fencing number, very protective but a little bulky. She's been meaning to make something smaller and sleeker, but her Anthro class is taking up all her time. That and intensive meditation to try to get rid of the ghost of the woman she murdered.

In her hands is a bared katana, its blade gleaming blood red in the moonlight.

"Stalking girls in the park?" she asks. "That's all the game you have? Not cool, bro."

He stares at her, and his unattended pants fall around his ankles. "Holy fu—"

Before the word is even out of the would-be mugger's mouth, she whirls and throws herself at him, moving gracefully through a world that slows around her. Even the raindrops float lazily down toward the earth, sliced neatly in two by her gleaming sword.

She smashes knee-first into his chest and knocks him staggering back. He crashes to earth like a dropped laundry basket, sending his phone into the air. She whirls around and cuts it neatly in half with her sword, sending the two pieces skittering among the damp grass.

Maybe it's the mask. She needs something scarier, maybe.

The mugger groans, his senses returning. He's just a kid, sporting a fashy sort of haircut—an undercut dyed blond on top, typical white nationalist/Nazi wannabe. She's honestly shocked he's not wearing a red Prather hat. Maybe she should have taken some pics of him in such a state with his own phone, rather than destroyed it.

Eh. Impulse.

The katana hungers. She can feel its terrible emptiness resonating through her arm. Driving her.

"That's that," she says. "Now—"

"Hello?" comes Lisa's voice.

Shit.

She ducks behind cover and looks around, and the mugger manages to pull away and draw his pants most of the way back up. He looks at the path, then at her, then at the path again.

Dammit. Stay. *Stay.*

The mugger doesn't. He seizes the opportunity and runs out of the bushes like a bat out of hell, limping as his pants slip, making the women scream in unison as he charges them. Svetlana— definitely that's her name, *God* she's hot—turns to run, but Lisa stands her ground, raises a can of pepper spray that she produced as soon as she sensed danger, and gives their unwelcome stalker a face-full of the stinking orange stuff. Or at least she would have, except that Svetlana yanks her away, and she ends up spraying it all over the perv instead. Enough gets on his face—over his nose and mouth—that he runs on, gargling and screaming, into the trees on the other side of the path.

Some of the spray gets on Yumi's mask before she can slip back behind a tree, and she instantly pushes it off her face before the stuff can seep through and give her more than a bad smell. Fortunately, Lisa and Svetlana are too distracted to see her. Avoiding being seen is her first priority, and she takes her job seriously.

She has to, after this crazy year.

Yumi Kujikawa expected college to be one thing but got something else entirely. Something way more exciting, but horrible, too. For instance, Megan, the first girl she crushed on in the dorms, hung herself under the influence of a doom cult in a spiritual echo of a dark cathedral next to the dorm, and after finding the body, Yumi absorbed Megan's spirit into the cursed family heirloom Muramasa katana. And she threatened to chop a speedster's feet off with the same sword, and the woman 100 percent believed that she would. The same sword she carries now, that hungers for the blood of the fool who dared to stalk female students.

Life as a superhero is fucking *weird.*

Ironically, patrol is one of the few times when things still make sense. The tutor her father hired, Sakuto, ran Yumi ragged on studying late into the night, so she bails every chance she gets to run around the park in her evolving costume. She really needs a new mask to pull it all together.

7

The stalker's pretty easy to follow, what with the screaming and choking, so Yumi runs through the night after him, Muramasa replaced in its scabbard but still burning. The moonlight is sparse, but it will have to do. Drawing the sword again doesn't seem like a good idea—she didn't even mean to draw it the first time.

Just a few months ago, she never drew her sword unless she was in real danger. Most of these street thug and stalker types don't count as danger, even if they have guns. With her powers, she can dodge bullets and suplex a creep before they get off more than a couple shots. These days, she draws the sword before she even makes the drop, and that scares them almost as much as it does her. Or at least it *should* scare her, Sakuto said, which always seemed like an exaggeration. Now, Yumi's starting to believe him.

The scream of a terrified man rings out in the woods ahead, and Yumi pulls up short. She puts her mask back on just in case, forgetting all about the pepper spray. Fortunately, it *is* just a funky smell.

Someone swooped in and took care of the issue, and she recognizes the signature terror.

Oh man.

A little further on, the mugger moans on the ground, staring at horrors no one else can see. Standing over him is a slim guy about her age, in baggy pants and a high-fashion blue and yellow hoodie. Neither flashy nor forgettable, the outfit sort of straddles the line between nice street clothes and a crime fighting costume. Street level. Chic. Very flattering.

They stare at one another, his hands wavering with some sort of distortion—as if the air has turned gelatinous—while her blade's flames slowly fade, leaving them in moonlight and the scattered light of a lamppost through the tree. One would think the bright colors would give him away in the moonlight, but there's a faded sort of aura about him, as if he isn't entirely there. Dark forces swirl, just at the edge of Yumi's perception, fading slowly from view.

"Muramasa," he says, his voice a little choked. Stiff.

Codenames. Right. "Ghost House," she replies.

Mark Obiyashi. Dammit.

This is the last thing she needs.

They were together for a while—or at least Yumi thought they were—and she isn't honestly sure what they are now. She's usually

8

pretty good with people, but around Mark, she's never been able to express herself (or, as she tried to explain to him once, able to "word good"). It's either awkward or adorable, depending on whom you ask, but always frustrating. It took Yumi three months to tell him how she really felt, and by that point, it was too late. She'd already loosed that arrow. Already done that deed. And a supervillain wasn't the only thing she killed that night.

God, he's staring at her. He wants her as much as she wants him. But neither of them can say it.

Awkward.

"Just, uh, out for patrol?" Mark asks. "Sorry to justice-steal, there."

That's funny. Laugh! Yumi tries to make herself laugh, but the best she can manage is an awkward sort-of cough. "I thought the park was mine on Tuesdays," she says.

"Uh." Mark clears his throat. "It's Wednesday."

"Oh," Yumi says. "Shit."

She knew that. They settled on a patrol routine over texts, to minimize the chances of a random encounter—you know, exactly like this. She has Tuesday, Thursday, and Saturday, while he has Monday, Wednesday, and Friday. Between Sensei Sakuto's rigorous schedule, training for Nationals, sleeping really badly, and all the rest of it, she must have lost track of time.

Unless she didn't, and her body put her in Mark's path.

Stupid body.

Yumi pulls out her phone and snaps a picture of the dude curled up on the ground in his damp boxers, gibbering in terror. This is a better picture than when she initially took him down. More hits on social media this way. She adds a waterfall tears filter. It seems fitting.

Mark looks over the mugger—basic street clothes, flashlight, no weapon, pants around his ankles—then at the sword at her belt. "Did—did you almost kill a peeping tom?"

"What? *Nooo*." Yumi can see her bright red eyes reflected in his black ones. "I mean, maybe."

"*Yumi*," he says. Admonishment. Compassion. Maybe a little warning.

"I thought we were using our made-up names."

He comes closer, his eyes intense in the half-light. Oh God, he's making a move. *Now* he's making a move. Shit. What should she do?

While Yumi considers, Mark comes up to her and takes hold of her mask. Black hairs catch in the edges and pinch, but she doesn't care. He pulls it off and drops it on the ground, while with his other hand he smooths a long lock of hair out of her face. The cool midnight air is soft on her cheeks. Her lips. His lips.

Then they're kissing.

Their bodies fit together so well, and Yumi wishes his touch didn't make her tingle all over. She wishes she didn't want him so badly. Because when they start kissing, hands exploring, hearts beating faster against each other—that's when it always happens. And this time is no exception.

She feels him stiffen, and not in a good way. Yumi tenses in reply and pulls free of his suddenly inert lips. Mark's face is ashen.

"She's here," Yumi says. "Isn't she?"

Mark's mouth works a little, but no words come out. He nods.

The Melting Woman.

It all comes crashing back then, and Yumi pulls away. She remembers the look on Killing Word's face. The feel of the arrow coming off the string. The way the villain's eyes widened as the arrow streaked toward her, breaking apart into five or six flesh-melting grenades. The horrified choking sound she made, trying but failing to scream. The smell, like burning pork and bleach.

Yumi can't see her most of the time—outside of nightmares, anyway—but Mark can. He *always* sees her. That's how his powers work. He sees ghosts, from the beautiful to the horrific, and the Melting Woman is the worst. And it's no surprise she haunts him when he gets close to Yumi, who's the reason the Melting Woman exists in the first place.

"I'm sorry," Mark says. "I don't—"

"No," Yumi says. "I shouldn't have let you do that. I shouldn't—"

He looks like she just kneed him in the gut. Dammit.

Yumi tears away from Mark and streaks off among the trees. Even without her heightened speed and augmented grace, she's much faster than him, and there's no way Mark will catch up.

And really, does he even want to?

She swiftly outdistances Mark and swings up into a tree. It's the same place she hid initially, actually, where she watched the stalker watch Lisa and the hot Russian girl trying to date her. There she hides, arms around her knees, and tries to tell herself she's crying because of the pepper spray on her mask. She tries not to hate herself.

It's really, really goddamn hard.

~

"Yumi?"

An hour later, Yumi perks up at the sound of her name.

It's Mark from somewhere nearby. Looking for her. She checks her phone, and she has half a dozen texts from him. She puts the phone back to sleep and sinks deeper into the shadows of the hollowed-out tree.

"Yumi?"

Part of her wants him to find her—to save her while there's still hope.

"Yumi?"

Part of her wonders if it's already too late.

CHAPTER 2

Baltimore, Maryland, Spring Break, 2018

"Yumi?"

She blinks her way into wakefulness. She dozed on the plane, and now everyone around her is standing, jostling to get their bags from the overhead bins, even though there's nowhere to go. They've landed in Baltimore, and that makes it time to hurry up and wait to get off the plane.

"Yumi?" Lisa Yamamoto looks worried, the way she usually looks. "You all right?"

"Oh." She stretches and finds only the usual aches. "Yeah. Fine. Why?"

"How'd you sleep through that landing?" Lisa asks. "We almost crashed. Like, there was *screaming*."

Not really a surprise. After all the supervillains she's fought with Justice or Something, Yumi can handle a rough landing. Particularly that time they had to blow up half a dozen robotic U.S. presidents; Taft packed a particular punch. Long story.

She and Lisa sit there, trapped in an odd space both private and public. Yumi is extremely aware of how close they are: their knees and shoulders touch, as they have for basically the whole flight to Baltimore. It was only an hour and half flight, and she shouldn't have slept at all, but she's been pulling extra-long training hours coupled with almost nightly patrols. Sleep is paramount to her training regimen, but Yumi's nerves have been frazzled leading up to the tournament and all that stuff with Mark and ... Well, the second Lisa casually leaned her head against Yumi's shoulder, she went right to sleep. It should have been sweet, but Yumi knows she has a tendency to talk in her sleep. She hopes she didn't say anything embarrassing.

"Lisa?"

"Yeah?"

Yumi bites her lip. "I—"

She feels it before it happens: a tremor in the air warning of incoming on her left side. It isn't precognition, exactly, but heightened reflexes: when her powers activate, the world seems to slow around her, allowing her to react to an attack as it unfolds. In this case, she slides closer to Lisa, practically straddling her on the seat, and deflects the falling duffel bag harmlessly into the seat back in front of her. It might have hit her head otherwise.

"Jeez!" comes the snide voice of Allory Greene, the dyed-blonde bombshell who's been sitting behind them during the flight. She's getting her carry-on down from overhead: a big PINK-brand sports bag. "You're such a spaz, Kujikawa."

"Yeah, spaz," says Samantha Oliver, the pinched-face brunette who's Allory's right-hand yes-woman. "They just told us, 'objects may have shifted during the flight,' remember?"

Yumi, her heart racing in reaction to the apparent threat, has no ready response, but Lisa pipes up instead. "Hey!" She comes out strong, but under Allory's mean-girl stare, she wilts back into her standard shyness. "Uh, just be careful, all right?"

"Whatever," Allory says. "When you two scissor-sisters are done groping each other, maybe you could move your bag, so it doesn't fall on me? Wouldn't want any injuries before nationals."

"Um." Yumi retreats from Lisa sheepishly, avoiding her gaze like a Whiteheart Twelve death ray. Paulette Bailey's in prison, sure, but she could still invent contact lenses that fired face-melting beams, right? Probably.

Sure enough, her own bag—a sleek black duffel, simpler but also more dependable than the monstrosity Allory totes around—hangs precariously, poised halfway over the aisle. Allory's second carry-on, which she made Samantha pretend was hers, is a massive pink roller, the colors perfectly matched and probably from the same set. This monstrosity has somehow clipped itself to the shoulder strap, so the more Yumi pulls, the closer it comes to falling. The nice septuagenarian lady across the aisle patiently awaiting her turn probably wouldn't appreciate either bag coming down on her head.

"Come on, yuppie girl." Allory puts her hands on her hips, casually striking a pose straight out of a fashion magazine. Yumi's never seen her go anywhere without a pink tracksuit opened just enough to expose a barely-there workout shirt and matching pink sports bra. Probably she bought this getup brand new for this event. "Get your shit."

Yumi takes a centering breath, just as Sakuto taught her, and surveys the tangle of clip and strap. As Sensei always says, it's worth taking a moment to plan before acting. Then she reaches up, zips Allory's bag closed so its contents won't spill all over them when she releases the bags, and finally undoes the clip. Allory is about to chide her, but Yumi gracefully retrieves the garish pink roller bag from the bin, her strong arms flexing, and draws up the handle for Allory to take. Then, quietly and gracefully, she sits back down next to Lisa, leaving Allory and Samantha standing awkwardly in the aisle with about six rows to empty before them.

"Are you all right?" Lisa asks.

Yumi nods absently, but she isn't really listening. She lays her hand on the black duffel, feeling the power simmering within. The Muramasa sword hungers. She hasn't fed it in a long time, and she doesn't plan to do so anytime soon. She wouldn't have even brought it to Nationals, but she knows the Factory is after it, and she doesn't trust it too far from her hands, let alone stashed somewhere in her dorm room.

Wouldn't Allory be freaked out if Yumi drew the katana out of her carry-on? It's definitely not the sort of thing that's supposed to be in the passenger cabin of an airplane, but Muramasa has a way of avoiding notice when it doesn't want to be seen, least of all by some overworked TSA agent performing security theater. It doesn't even set off metal detectors, for goodness sake. It's the perfect assassin's weapon ...

No. Stop thinking like that. That's just what Killdeer would want her to think.

Yumi feels Lisa's scrutiny and looks over just as Lisa locks away. "What?" she asks.

"It's 2018," Lisa says under her breath. "Who even says 'spaz'?"

That makes Yumi smile. It doesn't sound at all like the shy, retiring, avoid-confrontation-at-all-costs girl she met during orientation their first year. That girl loved anime and manga and all things kawaii, which Yumi found adorable. This girl is the same, but now she has a little bite to her that Yumi finds sexy as hell. Not that she can tell her that, of course.

The seat ahead of her shifts, and Yumi realizes the people ahead of them are getting up to go. Allory's face has gone red from her impatience, and she huffs.

"Move it, spaz," Allory says with a huff. "We've wasted enough time as it is." She rolls her eyes and storms off, massive roller bag bumping along behind her. Samantha hurries after, lugging her sports bag.

Yumi and Lisa share a look, and Lisa smiles a little. It lightens Yumi's heart, and only now does she realize that she needs this. Nationals are a vacation compared to all the drama in Cobalt City.

~

NCAA Nationals are everything Yumi expected and more. The bouts take place in a covered sporting arena surrounded on all sides by stands, which she suspects are used for basketball and concerts most of the time. A dozen mats with taped boundaries provide bouting space for fencers of all different shapes and sizes, genders and ethnicities, and weapon of choice, all of them made part of the same team by their nigh universal white tunics, masks, and gloves. Yumi didn't realize colorful lamés—the conductive jackets that pick up touches to score points—were becoming the norm. She always thought Allory was just being extra by wearing a pink one. The fencers' bare hands hint at their individuality—here a brown hand with pink flesh on the palm, there a set of painted and bejeweled nails—and the minute eccentricities of their uniforms, from affordable, sensible gear to high-end designer outfits from some of the most prestigious salons. Most competitors have their name stenciled in their school colors on their fencing knickers, but some also have tiny flairs on their masks or colorful lining on their gloves, demonstrating a bit of individuality that skirts the rules of competition.

Yumi's own gear comes from Leon Paul, plus a pair of black and pink piste sneakers hand-crafted in Italy just for her. Father doesn't exactly approve of his little girl taking up fencing, but damned if he's not going to make sure she has the best equipment imaginable. Her uniform is pure white, of course, as compared to her accustomed jet-black kendo outfit. The duality amuses her, mostly because fencing, at least the way she does it, hardly seems like the sort of thing a snow-white princess would do, while kendo feels much more meditative and peaceful.

The one part of her uniform that isn't shiny and new is her glove: a much worn, slightly discolored left-hand glove she inherited from her mother. This is the glove Kujikawa Eiko would have worn at the 2000 Summer Olympics, if Yumi hadn't been born just that previous December. She almost competed anyway, but the pregnancy had messed up her training regimen, and Eiko had needed time to recover. Little did she know that would be her last chance.

Open qualifiers for saber take up the majority of the first day, and the arena is full of clashing blades, point sensors buzzing, and exhalations of effort, jubilant victory cries, and growls of defeat Even coming straight from the airport, the team from Cobalt City University barely got there in time to register by the nine a.m. cutoff.

"Sorry, sorry, sorry," Lisa had said on the shuttle over. "I got the schedule wrong!"

Allory gave her a hard time about it, but Yumi stuck up for her as best she could. At least they made it.

It's a good thing they did, because Nationals is a blast. Foil started the previous day, before they arrived, but no one on the CCU team fights foil. Saber starts at ten, and Yumi's suited and ready by then. Epee qualifiers are tomorrow morning, so Samantha and Allory abscond to elsewhere, no doubt to gossip and snark.

Throughout the morning, Yumi fights a number of bouts, working out the kinks from the plane until her body feels warm and loose. She handily qualifies for the top sixty-four, though Sun Teng from Oregon gives her some trouble with some really explosive movement and expert timing. Yumi thinks Teng will at least make the quarter-finals, easy.

Her other bouts don't attract a lot of attention—just good, solid fencing against skilled fencers. During the bout with a girl from Vermont, there's a commotion that goes up on the other side of the arena floor, which is so loud and distracting that she misses a riposte and gives up a point she shouldn't have. Still, good bouts, and they promise good things for the future.

At noon, she's sitting with Lisa in their team's section, mercifully spared Allory and Samantha's company. Yumi slouches in one of the seats, one leg stretching up over the arm, munching on a protein bar and watching the rest of the bouts finish up. By contrast, a couple seats full of luggage away, Lisa sits very straight and proper, eating what looks like a bento she must have brought from home. Where did she get that? Yumi's stomach gurgles.

"Lisa," she says, exactly as Lisa is starting to speak too. They both stop, start again, then stop.

"You, uh, you first," Lisa says.

"Any word from Coach?"

Lisa shakes her head. "No update." Their coach missed the flight, then followed up with an email that he had come down with a bad stomach bug and that she, Lisa, was in charge. That was quite a task to put on her slim shoulders, but Lisa is, without a doubt, the most responsible of all of them.

"I ... I'm checking the scores. This StarPad isn't getting updates. The WiFi is real spotty."

"Shit, that's more Janella's thing," Yumi says. Though if her tech whiz teammate heard her say something like that, she'd probably go ballistic. Possibly literally, if she brought her mech suit with her.

"I'll go find the IT desk." Lisa holds up her bento box. "You, uh, can have the rest of this, if you want. I ate all the meaty parts." She blushes a little. "I mean, since you're vegan and all."

"Oh. Thanks."

Lisa heads off, leaving Yumi alone in her team section. The other teams, all of whom seem to have brought more members than CCU, are scattered all around her on this side of the arena. She tries to smile at one or two of the others, but to no avail.

"Kujikawa." One of the Nationals staff, a good-looking twenty-something in uniform approaches their section of the stands. He refers closely to his own StarPad, which doesn't seem to have WiFi issues. "Kujikawa, Yumi? From Cobalt City U?"

"That's me," she says, looking up from the protein bar she's busy devouring. "Kujikawa Yumi!"

He frowns in confusion. "What?" he asks, and there's a classic southern drawl to the word.

"Because I'm Japanese and we say our family name first, then—" She's clearly lost him. "You know what? Never mind. Am I up?"

18

"Women's round of sixty-four starts this afternoon." He nods. "Marks, Janine," he says. "Stanford and ... Oregon Fencing Alliance?"

"Here!" A dark-skinned young woman, probably a junior or senior, raises her hand and steps forward. She has the classic saber build—stocky, thick, and compact—wears beads in her locs, and looks determined. She's also a lefty, as most high-level competitors are.

"The OFA?" That perks Yumi's interest.

"Next up, round of sixty-four saber, piste number three, one p.m." The attendant checks the time on his tablet. "Twenty minutes." He heads off to alert the next fencers.

The two young women shake hands politely and head toward the locker room together.

"You're from the OFA?" Yumi asks. "But you go to Stanford?"

"I transferred from Portland State," she says. "But I'm still repping my hometown, you know?"

"Totally." Yumi likes her. "Do you know Mariel Zagunis? She's awesome."

"Oh yeah." Janine grins with very white teeth. "She teaches at the club all the time. Not like my trainer, but I've taken some lessons from her." She furrows her brow. "Kujikawa. You related to Eiko Kujikawa? You know—" She leans in close. "Silver Sakura?"

"My—" Yumi feels a spark of heat in her stomach. She nods reverently. "My mother."

"Damn, girl," Janine says. "This is gonna be tough. Good luck."

"You too."

Lisa appears. "Hey! Uh." Her enthusiastic look fades, and she looks awkwardly away as Janine and Yumi finish up their conversation. They part ways, Janine heading toward the other end of the locker room with her coach to strategize while she gets ready, and Yumi turns to Lisa.

"Hey. What's up, Manager?"

Lisa is still watching Janine's retreating back sidelong, but she shakes it off. "I, uh, got the seed chart, and, uh, there's something you should see."

Yumi scans the saber rankings, unsure at first what Lisa means. Sixty-four names in the double-elimination tournament. She recognizes a few of the names: Emily Dobrova, Anastacia

Matthews, Sun Teng, Janine Marks ... Yumi's bout with Janine is apparently the only one she has until Thursday. Apparently, her second opponent qualified but unexpectedly withdrew from the competition, so she has a bye on Wednesday. Then she sees it.

"Allory qualified in saber?" Yumi frowns. She hadn't been paying attention to the qualifiers, except to her own scores. "I thought she was here for epee. I always beat her at saber."

"She did pretty well in the qualifiers," Lisa says. "Qualified fiftieth percentile on points. Only lost one bout, to someone named—"

"With saber? Allory Greene?" Yumi shakes her head. "I had no idea she was so determined to humiliate herself against me."

"Well," Lisa says. "Maybe she's hoping someone else will beat you?"

They both chuckle at that. Yumi only ever fought one swordswoman who could beat her: Danielle Swain, international assassin and not the sort of person who'd compete at a petty fencing tournament. Yumi first faced her when the mysterious Factory, which wanted to recruit Yumi, tracked her down at CCU. Danielle had come to test her or kill her—she's not sure which—and Yumi had narrowly made it out, mostly because she had help. Not that she's told anyone outside Justice or Something about any of that, let alone Lisa.

Lisa bolts upright and snaps a fake salute. "Urgent message for Akame!"

Yumi has to smile at the inside joke, delivered when she least expects it. Lisa really is adorable.

"Are you ok?" Lisa asks.

Yumi nods. "Sure am. Just spaced there for a second. You?"

"Totally," Lisa says. "What would I have to be worried about? I'm not the one fighting the best collegiate fencers in the country on her epic quest to take on the finest fencers in the world! For the glory of America!"

She says it with enough shonen energy to make Yumi giggle.

"You could be worried about *me*, you know."

Lisa smiles shyly. "I never worry about you."

~

20

At one p.m., Yumi squares off for her bout with Janine Marks, both of them sleekly attired in flawless white aside from their knickers stenciled in their school colors: "Marks" is in cardinal red and black on white, "Kujikawa" in blue and gray. Both their lamés are metallic gray. They salute each other in elegant, formalized movements. Janine's style of salute is tight and efficient, with no extra flourishes to show off. This tells Yumi something about her as a fencer: that she can expect a well-practiced form that leaves little room for error. She can deal with a fencer like that.

The arena is pretty empty on this, the first day of Nationals, which is good, because Yumi isn't used to performing with an audience. A few looky-loos and fencing enthusiasts are in the stands, but mostly it's the other teams, who number a few hundred fencers plus various coaches, team managers, and hangers on. She can feel Allory's challenging glare, but that's not any different from a regular practice. Only one person makes her anxious, and that's Lisa Yamamoto, who is watching her with hands clasped anxiously in front of her.

They take up their dueling postures, Janine adopting an overhand, hanging guard, while Yumi goes with a low guard more like a kendo fencer. It's way shorter and less defensively sound, but she likes the flexibility and unpredictability of the posture, because her saber can go any number of ways, while a hanging guard mostly cuts down or across. With her speed, Yumi is confident she can parry or avoid the first attack in almost any exchange.

She turned down her coach's suggestion to study up on her potential opponents—watch videos of them, analyze their style, come up with strategies. If she gets too much in her head, she'll make a mistake.

Janine's form is erect and strong, all of her potential energy stored up in her core, ready to surge forward or backward in equal balance. Yumi expects she'll fight as mechanically well, too.

Which is exactly what happens on the first pass, as no sooner does the judge say "fence!" then Janine explodes out of the starting position at Yumi, advancing like a madwoman. Yumi expected something more cautious—testing her style, getting a feel for her instincts—but the quick advance is not that. And then when Janine gets close enough, she tenses her legs and explodes forward in a leaping advance while slashing. It's almost like a flèche, though of course those aren't possible in saber: it's forbidden to cross the back foot in front of the forward foot, but Janine drives herself forward whilst keeping her feet in the proper order, like a charging balestra.

Yumi tries to parry, but Janine's sword disengages expertly under her guard and snakes in toward her face. She barely retreats fast enough to avoid Janine running into her, and instead the blade drags across the top of her right arm. Anyone else, Yumi thinks that attack would have got them in the head.

"Halt!" the judge says, even as the indicator beeps. "Touch, Marks."

The assembled audience gasps, their reaction seemingly belated because the attack was so fast, and descends into murmurs.

The first pass, and Yumi gave up a touch.

Janine backs off, smiling at her under the mask. A unique move, right out of the gate. What a way to start the match.

Yumi feels a flare of heat inside herself: Muramasa calls to her from her bag, only twenty feet away, under Lisa's feet at the team area. She doesn't need the sword, though. She can win this totally on her own.

Besides, Janine wants her off-balance, and that's a losing strategy.

They head back to on guard and wait while the judges confer about Janine's off-the-wall attack. Yumi sees nothing wrong with it, though, and ultimately the judges bear out her opinion.

The second pass starts, and Janine doesn't try any sort of wild, leaping attack. She approaches more cautiously the second time, saber flicking into different vectors as she seeks a weakness. Some people say fencing is like chess, some say it's like rock-paper-scissors, and the trick is, they're all correct. It's a complex web of intuition, strategy, reflex, and commitment, all wrapped into just a few seconds, if that.

As they both advance, Yumi feels the world around her start to slow, but she lunges forward before her powers can take effect.

Janine, caught off guard, steps back as she extends into Yumi's thrust, and their touch alarms go off almost simultaneously. Yumi wins the touch, because she had the right of way, barely, but that was clumsy.

She really needs to get the hang of this.

The third pass, Yumi falls into the rhythms of practice at CCU. It's much easier to avoid using her powers there, where the pressure is way less, but the familiar techniques and thought patterns calm her. She forces herself to take three deep breaths between each pass, and the world quiets outside of "fence," "touch, Marks" or "touch, Kujikawa," and "halt!" She looks at nothing but Janine and her saber. She pushes the fire out of her mind and focuses on good technique, setting strong parries, and committing to direct attacks. It pays off, because even without actively using her powers, she's faster than Janine, and she throws herself into attacks that would be reckless if she weren't so well-trained. Sensei Sakuto would approve of her focus.

She wins the next three touches, not really through any awesome moves or anything, just solid fencing, and then they mostly trade hits for the rest of the first round, and the score ends at seven to six, Yumi. It's a standard scoring scheme: first fencer to fifteen touches, or most touches after three rounds of three minutes each. That doesn't seem all that long, but it feels like an eternity when you're actually doing it.

Janine's coach comes to talk with her during the break, efficiently giving her tips and insights, and Yumi—who has no coach to talk to—resists the urge to attune her ears to overhear. Her powers have grown over the last six months, and she's not sure if her improved hearing is entirely natural. She'd determined not to cheat. To win this fairly.

In round two, Yumi attacks into a really excellent parry, and the riposte slaps her wrist hard enough to knock the saber out of her hand. Worse, the weapon comes unclipped and drags along the piste half a step before Yumi's even aware of what happened. The judge calls "halt!" to stop them as Yumi stands there, unarmed, against a saber sweeping around to hit her again for good measure. Janine stops short, though, with the blade about three inches from the side of Yumi's mask. The moment stretches, and then Janine pulls back, taking her saber out of line. Disarming is a significant issue, and fencers are most likely to get hurt in that moment than most of the bout. As soon as a disarmed weapon hits the ground, the point is over, so if Janine hit Yumi with that follow-up attack, it would just be bad sportsmanship. As it is, the slap to the wrist before the disarm gives Janine a point.

Janine steps forward before they set up for the next pass. "You all right?"

If she was wielding Muramasa, nothing could have disarmed her.

Yumi pushes the thought away. "Totally."

They shake off-hands, then Yumi slides her toe under the saber and flips it back into her hand with a flourish. That draws applause from the crowd, and Yumi sees Lisa standing there, clapping. The disarm requires a complete reset and testing of the system, to make sure both their lamés are conducting the touch of their respective weapons, and it delays the rest of the bout. This is the kind of tedium that Yumi least enjoys about fencing. She wants to be back in the fray.

There, in the audience, she sees something that chills her blood. A pair of eyes, yellow like those of a wolf, illumined in the light of a cell phone. Yumi blinks and looks again, but she sees no one unusual. It must have been her imagination. She hopes.

At the beginning of the next pass, Janine comes at her with a wild attack, maybe getting tired after the long bout, and Yumi ducks her attack and cuts below her arm, catching the bottom edge of her jacket. It barely looks like a hit, but the sensor goes off, and it's twelve to ten. That score remains at the end of round two. Pretty close.

It's been a great match so far. Yumi wanted to get it all done by the end of round two, but she's lost herself a bit in the match, and hasn't been fencing tactically. She's letting herself have fun, and maybe she wants to drag it out.

Round three starts, and by that point, Yumi has got a really good sense of Janine's style. She wins the next two touches no problem, taking a total of about thirty seconds to make it happen.

On the next pass, Janine comes in for a high attack, but she's wary enough to keep her body back. Fluidly, Yumi shifts into a high guard, parries her saber, and turns her wrist to both throw Janine's saber off the line of attack and drag her own saber across the lower half of her mask. If they were using real swords and no masks, that riposte would have cut Janine's throat. The move is flawless and so fast that it stuns the audience to silence even as the sensor goes off, the judge calls a halt, then announces Yumi's victory.

Yumi continues her momentum and ends up facing the judges, where she half-bows, saber out wide, which draws even more enthusiasm, even cheers. She sees Lisa smiling big.

It's a pretty spectacular bout to start the women's saber track at Nationals, and Yumi has won fifteen to ten.

"I thought I had you for a minute there," Janine says when they meet to shake hands. "Good match."

"Yeah." Yumi grins at her. "You're great. Good luck moving forward."

"You too."

When she gets to the locker room, Lisa is there, waiting, absorbed in her phone.

"Hey," Yumi says, still energetic from the bout. It seems weird to gear down after just the one bout, but she's finished for the day. She's already in the round of sixteen. She strips off her lamé, jacket, and plastron—the underarm protector worn under the jacket. Then she loosens the straps and pulls off her plastic chest protector with an audible pop. "Did you see that? That was such a good bout." Yumi pulls off her piste shoes, tossing them haphazardly next to her bag. "Janine's real good."

Lisa murmurs a non-committal reply.

"God, I need a shower." Yumi stops by one of the sinks to pop out the blue contact lenses she's been wearing since this morning. Her red eyes can distract an opponent, and if she ever accidentally uses her powers, the glowing would be a dead giveaway. "Everything ok in social media land?"

"Oh." Lisa shakes herself. "Sure, yeah."

Yumi, down to her sports bra and athletic pants, peers over Lisa's shoulder. "What's up?"

Startled, the girl stiffens and presses the phone to her stomach, turning to Yumi. Their eyes meet. They're suddenly much closer than either of them intended, and Lisa's cheeks flush bright red.

"Sorry," Yumi says. "I didn't mean to scare you."

"I'm—I'm not scared." Lisa briefly looks at Yumi's chest, then makes a point of looking her right in the eye. "You, uh, weren't you going to take a shower?"

Yumi grins. "Yeah, of course."

She discards the rest of her clothes as she heads over to the shower, sure that Lisa is still watching her. She's so cute when she's flustered.

The water is warm and soothing, but Yumi can't really relax. She feels wired, excited, and ready for action. But according to the list Lisa showed her earlier, she only has the one bout today, none tomorrow, then two on Thursday. The semis will be Friday, with the finals on Saturday. She's hopeful that she'll be in the winner's bracket all week.

"What are you looking up?" Yumi asks as she scrubs herself down. "Did new leaks about that Supergroup biopic drop or something?"

They've discussed the upcoming Supergroup movie extensively and compared notes on the role the heroines on the team played in their respective queer awakenings. For Yumi, it was Lady Vengeance, obviously, but for Lisa, it was Athena, which reflects a more structured kind of sapphic interest. And this new movie's supposed to star Athena's daughter, Angel DeSantes—the superheroine A-Girl—as her mother in the film, and upon whom Lisa confessed to having a massive crush. Yumi wonders how Lisa would react if she knew that Yumi took Angel to senior prom back in Seattle. It wasn't a date or anything—as far as she knows, Angel's straight—but how much would Lisa's head explode?

They're also professionally affiliated; Muramasa and A-Girl have teamed up a couple times. Not that Yumi can really tell Lisa about that, since she's not out about her secret identity. In fact, there's a *lot* Lisa doesn't know about her.

Yumi feels hot all over—frustrated—and what she'd really like is someone to join her in the shower. Honestly, being naked, excited, and only a few feet from Lisa isn't the easiest thing to deal with, so she resists the urge to draw out the shower. Once she's cleaned off, she shuts off the water, realizing only then that she didn't wash her hair. Eh, it's probably fine.

When she gets out, Lisa's looking at the phone again, her brow furrowed. This time, Yumi resolves to get a look. She adjusts the towel around herself and heads over, sure Lisa can see her out of the corner of her eye.

"What's up?" she asks.

"Have you seen this?" Lisa passes the phone over.

It's a video, posted on Twitter by the Flasher, a notorious right-wing TMZ sort of organization, with about a thousand likes and half as many retweets. It mentions only one handle, and that's the USA Fencing official account. It's dark and not a very good video—it looks like a Go-Pro recording from some guy running through the park. At first, she's about to dismiss it as nothing, but then she sees a distinctive red flash in the dark, and then a silhouette she can't help but recognize.

Jesus. That's *her*.

Fire roils at the pit of her stomach, and she realizes that her sword hungers. She becomes acutely aware of having not fed it for entirely too long. It needs to kill—to feast.

"Isn't that Muramasa?" Lisa asks.

"Um," Yumi says, unable to think straight. "Who?"

"You know, the ninja girl on Justice or Something?"

"Uh." Yumi reels. "I don't ... I don't really follow that sort of thing."

"Really? She's really cool, and I'm pretty sure she goes to our school—"

"You know," Yumi says, covering Lisa's hand—and the phone—with her own. "I'm really tired. Let's go check out the hotel, huh?"

Lisa blinks at her. "Sure."

In her well-secured locker, Muramasa burns. It hungers, but not so much Yumi can't ignore it. She's managed to avoid feeding it this long. Surely she can keep it up.

What could go wrong?

CHAPTER 3

When they finally get to the Baltimore Marriott around 5 p.m., Allory and Samantha are ahead of them at the front desk and have clearly been there for several minutes. A luggage cart full of pink suitcases and Samantha's kind of forlorn purple bag creaks next to them under the weight. Allory is slurping on a huge iced coffee drink of some kind while the poor Black woman behind the desk listens to her condescending ramble with a long-suffering expression. Yumi can't help but feel for her.

"Hey," Yumi says, not in genuine greeting but at least to draw aggro. Give Allory a different target than the harried attendant.

It works and gets exactly the sort of reaction she expects. "Hey yourself, Kujikawa," Allory says. "I see you're taking your time getting back, just like you did in your match."

"It worked, didn't it?" Yumi asks.

Allory doesn't have a suitable comeback for that and just sniffs derisively.

Samantha gives her a good glare, one that makes Lisa stiffen at Yumi's side.

"Ok, that should do it," the receptionist says. "Room 901. Do you need—"

"Just the ninth floor?" Allory rolls her eyes. "You don't have anything higher up? The farther away from this filthy city the better."

"You requested two beds, the best view, and a corner room," the receptionist says. "If you're willing to take something else—"

"No, that's all non-negotiable." Allory laughs mirthlessly and looks pointedly at Yumi and Lisa. "We're not *lesbians.*"

That makes Lisa stiffen again, and Yumi bites her tongue.

"I'm sorry, ma'am." The woman smiles through her teeth. "There aren't any better rooms, unless you want the presidential suite. That's—" She clicks some keys and turns her screen toward Allory to show her a price.

Allory's gaze flicks to Yumi, who pointedly keeps her expression neutral. "Fine. 901 it is."

"Great." The receptionist types a few more commands. "And how many keys will you be needing?"

"Two, obviously. I'll need a spare."

"Um." Samantha perks up. "What about me?"

"Oh." Allory rolls her eyes. "Three keys, I guess."

Yumi lays a hand on Lisa's arm. "You all right?"

"I'm fine." Lisa blushes and looks away. It was probably Allory's mildly homophobic jab. Lisa's not in the closet or anything, but she doesn't make a big thing of it at school, let alone here in a strange city with a stranger. And it's obviously incredibly rude.

"And will you be needing help up to your room?" the receptionist asks.

"Well, I'm not going to carry my own bags, obviously."

"Well, bless your heart." She rings a bell: one of those old fashioned "ring bell for service" bells. Yumi can see in the purposeful way that she does it, with a little smile, that something else is going on, and when a bellhop doesn't immediately appear, she gets it.

Yumi's smiling a little when they step up to the desk.

"How can I help you?" the receptionist says. "Y'all part of the same group?"

"Yes, Cobalt City University," Yumi says. "Kujikawa. That's K-U-J..."

"There you are," the receptionist says. "Yumi? That's pretty."

"Thanks." Yumi checks her nametag. "Ysaora? That's beautiful."

"You got it on the first try." The woman looks at her appraisingly. "Not many do."

"I feel that."

Ysaora looks at Lisa, who perks up, startled. "Oh, uh, Lisa Yamamoto." She fumbles her wallet out of her purse, then tries to squeeze her ID out of the faux leather case. "Sorry, uh..."

"It's fine, honey," Ysaora says. "I just need to see it."

30

They show her their IDs. Yumi sneaks a glance over at Allory some ten feet away, who is starting to get annoyed at waiting for the bellhop who isn't coming, and Samantha, who is absorbed in her phone.

Ysaora keeps tapping away. "I'm sorry," she says. "I had you booked for adjoining rooms, since y'all are on the same team, but Ms. Greene wanted to upgrade—"

"Totally ok." The last thing Yumi needs is to be neighbors with Allory and Samantha. "Is the room still available?"

"Yes, but—" The woman furrows her brow. "It's a King room."

"Oh."

"Something wrong?" Lisa asks. She's only been paying partial attention.

Allory, on the other hand, brightens at the news. "I'm sure they only need the *one* bed," she says with a cruel smile.

What are you, twelve? Yumi thinks but doesn't say. Lisa looks like she's approaching an aneurysm, and the last thing Yumi needs is for this to turn into a scene. "Are there any rooms with two beds?" she asks.

"I'll check." The receptionist chews on her lip. "We're pretty full, with the competition in town, you know."

The bellhop has finally arrived: a nondescript guy in his twenties, who immediately becomes the new target of Allory's frustrated wrath. He's white, though, so she's a little more tempered in her barbs. Not that Allory would ever admit to being racist. She's from California—she doesn't "see color."

Now that Allory and Samantha are safely enclosed in the elevator, everyone can breathe a sigh of relief, but the grossness still infects the lobby. The few white people are either oblivious or doing their best to look inconspicuous. One guy looks upset, which might be a good sign, but Yumi sees his red ballcap and knows it's the opposite.

"Um, sorry about our teammate," Lisa says. "She's—"

Ysaora brightens. "Oh, it's fine, honey," she says. "I'm used to it."

"Yeah." Yumi narrows her eyes after Allory and her string of entitled bullshit. No one should have to be *used* to that. "Hey, you said the presidential suite was open?"

The receptionist looks at Yumi over her glasses. "Yes?"

"Put us there." She slips a black credit card out of her wallet and slides it across the counter.

Ysaora looks at her quizzically, then down at the card. Her eyes widen behind her big glasses. "Oh," she says. "Is this ... I'm going to need to see your ID again, Miss."

"Of course." Yumi pulls out her Washington State driver's license. "Two keys, please."

Lisa blinks at Yumi. "What is happening right now?" she asks in a whisper.

The receptionist shakes her head in disbelief. "Um, thank you, Miss Kujikawa," she says. "Will you be needing anything else? There's a massage package, or, uh, I can unlock the minibar—oh, sorry, uh, I see you're not twenty-one, Miss—"

"Yumi is fine." Her shoulder aches a little. "Though a massage *does* sound nice. Any openings today?" She checks her phone for the time. "Around six, maybe? Female masseuse, obviously."

"I'll see if I can book that," the receptionist says, typing furiously. Clearly, she's got a lot of coordination and scrambling to do, and she's stalling for time. "Any other spa packages? Facial? Mani pedi?"

Yumi looks over at Lisa, who's staring at her, utterly bewildered. "Is there some sort of deluxe, combination package? Full pampering." She leans across to whisper confidentially. "You know, the sort of thing basic white girls like my really rude friend try to schedule on a whim?"

"Oh." Ysaora returns her smile. "Well ... there *is* a three-hour cleanse, deep tissue massage, and beauty treatment, followed by a cheese and wine tasting, if you're interested—not that you'd want the wine," she says, in a way that makes it clear they can have the wine anyway. "It's too late today, but the first available appointment is nine a.m. tomorrow. I'll just have to clear the spa of other appointments—"

"That sounds great," Yumi says.

"But—" Lisa finally manages to speak. "Won't the glove just mess up your nails anyway?"

Yumi smiles at her. "Oh, it's not for *me*."

Wide-eyed, Lisa utters a little "eep!" It's only the most adorable thing Yumi's seen all day.

"I'll just reschedule this—" The receptionist types with a little satisfied smile. "There. There's a spa menu up in the room, and any other amenities you might want. Let me call someone to take your bags."

"Oh, it's fine." Yumi hefts her fencing bag over her shoulder. "We got it."

"Ok, Yumi." The receptionist smiles. "Fourteenth floor. And you call the front desk if you need anything. Anything at all. Just ask for Yzzie."

"I will, Yzzie. Thanks."

In the elevator, Lisa stares at her, utterly lost. "The presidential suite?"

"Apparently." Yumi presses one of their keycards to the sensor and hits the buttons for "9" and "PH."

The elevator stops on the ninth floor and opens briefly—long enough for the bellhop from the lobby to see them, smile, and murmur something about taking the next one. Behind him, they see Allory and Samantha in the hallway, both of them staring at their phones in disbelief.

"What do you *mean* my treatment is cancelled for tomorrow?" Allory says. "What—"

The elevator dings, the doors shut again, and they ascend once more.

"Did—" Lisa asks. "Did you do that? On purpose?"

"What? No." Yumi smiles wryly. "Maybe."

"Oh. My. God." Lisa looks shocked. "You're *bad*."

"The worst."

Lisa stifles a giggle.

~

The elevator dings at the PH floor into a miniature lobby, well-appointed and decorated with tasteful art of landscapes and still-life images of fruit and various desserts. There's only one room on this floor, marked with fine oak double-doors, and they open into a palatial suite bigger than most apartments in Cobalt City. A massive fruit basket, obviously thrown together on short notice but overflowing with apples, oranges, grapes, nuts, and other snacks, sits on the sturdy table under a miniature chandelier that probably cost as much as their flight here.

Lisa looks around, marveling at the huge suite. "I mean, I knew you were rich," she says. "I guess I didn't realize you were *that* rich."

"*Father* is that rich," Yumi says. "It's kind of embarrassing, really."

Lisa purses her lips and looks shyly over at her. "Room service rich?"

"Sure." Yumi grins. "I'm starving."

They order—Lisa can't decide, so Yumi orders the five vegetarian things on the menu to share—then explore the massive suite while they're waiting. It has its own kitchen and living room, with plush couches, a massive TV, and even an electric fireplace. Yumi amuses them both by shifting through the various display options, from orange to blue flames to ... neon pink hearts? They laugh and turn that off.

The bathroom is like a spa unto itself, the whole place tiled for a walk-in shower with no door. There's a jacuzzi so big they don't ever need to use the hotel hot tub, and two sinks set apart by well-stocked cabinets with every bathroom appliance they could want. Just going through them all is a source of fun, and they spend ten minutes quizzing each other about what each gadget is supposed to do.

They're in there for so long, room service arrives, and Yumi heads back to let them in. It's the same guy who helped Allory and Samantha to their room, and he smiles ingratiatingly at her as he pushes a cart of dishes covered with metal lids into the room.

Ysaora is there too, all smiles. "Just making sure the room is sufficient for your needs."

"I think so, Yzzie, thanks." Yumi lifts one of the lids and inspects the steaming veggie risotto. Her stomach gurgles. "This doesn't have dairy, right?"

"As instructed, Miss Kuj—Yumi."

She smiles. "Make sure to put a tip on the room," she says.

The bellhop's eyes widen but he doesn't say anything.

Ysaora nods. "How, uh, how much, Miss Yumi?"

"Whatever you think is reasonable."

"Oh." Ysaora nods. "Uh, ten percent? Twenty?"

"Make it forty, and you've got a deal."

When Ysaora and the bellhop are gone, Yumi realizes she's alone.

"Lisa?" she calls.

She finds Lisa in the bedroom, its sliding glass doors and balcony overlooking the bay. It offers a pretty fantastic view—the sunrise is going to be amazing—but that isn't what Lisa is staring at.

The bed is huge. It looks like someone shoved two king-size beds together. It even has posts at the four corners where someone might hang curtains. And Lisa is just standing at the foot of the bed, trembling slightly as though facing down some sort of cosmic monster or kaiju or maybe just a huge bed that will swallow her up if she looks away from it.

Carelessly, Yumi flops down onto the bed, which feels marvelously comfortable after a day of travel, fighting, and dealing with intensely unpleasant blonde teammates. She lets out a long, relaxed sigh and gazes out the window at the birds flying past as the light drains from the sky.

"It's not too ostentatious, is it?" Yumi asks. "I mean, it *is* a little ostentatious, but—"

"That's, um, that's a big bed," Lisa says, chewing her lip. "The, uh, *only* bed."

"Shit, you're right." Yumi didn't even think of that. Her cheeks feel warm, and she sits back up. "You take it. I'll probably just meditate anyway, or I can call Yzzie for a roll-away." She starts to climb off the bed. "You know, that couch does look really—"

"No, I—" Lisa smiles meekly. "We can share."

Yumi didn't expect that. "Are—are you sure?"

"Yes." Lisa looks determined. "I mean, look how *big* this thing is."

"It *is* big."

"We can't just waste this."

"I guess we can't."

She sits down next to Yumi, very proper and a little bit tense, and looks out the window with her. She's fidgeting with her hands, like she's working up to saying something but hasn't yet got up the nerve.

"What's wrong?" Yumi asks.

"Nothing, it's just—" Lisa looks at her and gives her an awkward little smile. "It's just ... a lot."

"Too much?" Yumi asks. "I ... I didn't mean to make you feel uncomfortable or anything."

"No, it's not that," Lisa says. "You're just ... a little intimidating. With all the money, and the swords, and the red eyes—"

"Shit." Yumi had taken out her contacts after the bout with Janine and completely forgot about them. "I can put my contacts back in—"

She starts to get up, but Lisa catches her wrist. She doesn't look at her, but rather out the window.

Slowly, Yumi sits back down.

"It's just how you are," Lisa says. "You're so strong. I ... I just feel *small* around you."

"What?" Yumi looks over at her, horrified. "You ... No, this will not stand."

Lisa blinks in confusion. "Huh?"

Yumi pulls her to her feet, and they stand there, eye to eye. Yumi squints, considering.

"What?" Lisa asks again.

"You are a totally normal sized person," Yumi says. "In fact, I think you're taller than me."

Lisa blushes. "No, I'm not—" Then she looks—really looks—and can't help but smile. "Oh my God, I think I *am*."

"Well, you don't have to rub it in," Yumi says, and they both laugh.

Yumi falls onto the bed, laughing, and Lisa flops down right next to her. They're both laughing now, deep fits that originate from deep down—what Sensei Sakuto would call "laughing from the heart of the mountain."

Only then do they realize they're still holding hands—first looking down, then meeting each other's gaze. Neither makes a move to let go, however. In fact, Yumi adjusts her grip and squeezes Lisa's hand, making her smile.

There's a discreet knock at the door.

"That's ... probably the masseuse," Yumi says.

"Oh." Lisa covers her mouth with her hand. She looks embarrassed. "I forgot about the masseuse."

They share a smile.

Yumi really, really wants to kiss Lisa right now. Her lips look so warm and inviting. Lisa's dark eyes are unreadable, and her lip trembles slightly. Does she want—?

The knock at the door comes again, and Yumi winces.

"We should probably get that," Lisa says.

36

"Agreed."

~

That night, Yumi dreams of fire—fire, and the Melting Woman.

The ghost stands in the shadows of the room, looking down at Yumi as she lies there, trying to sleep. She's a silhouette more than a person, and when Yumi tries to see her, the Melting Woman's visage makes her eyes fall out of focus. Yumi knows it's her, though. She'll never forget that face, or the way it fell apart even as she looked at it. She's never seen the ghost, though. Was this what Mark always saw when they were together?

"I'm sorry," she says. "I don't know what you want."

The Melting Woman lifts her arm, which drips as though wet. Bits of flesh and blood slip off her amorphous limb, her fingers sliding apart and curling downward.

Yumi sits bolt upright, calling on Muramasa, but it doesn't come. The power is cut off—she is alone.

The Melting Woman takes half a dozen juddering steps toward Yumi, only to slide apart into multiple gelatinous chunks that wobble to the floor and start melting through it. Last is her face, which sloughs off as she leans toward Yumi, mouth open wide in a cry of rage ...

Then Yumi is awake, Lisa shaking her. "Yumi?" she says. "Yumi! Are you all right?"

"What—what happened?" Yumi manages to ask. She looks at the slimy blood trail the Melting Woman left across the room, but there's nothing there—only the darkened hardwood floor.

"You were having a nightmare, I think," Lisa said. "You ... you looked like your hair was on fire."

Yumi blinks. "What?"

"No, it's—it's nothing," Lisa says. "Are you ok?"

"Yeah. I think so."

Lisa cuddles up next to her and goes back to sleep, but Yumi lies there a long time, staring at the corner of the room, wondering if the shadows are a figure watching her.

CHAPTER 4

The first day for saber at Nationals had some excellent fencing and no major upsets or scandals. There were the normal share of close calls, but only a couple of good-spirited challenges of judgments. Electrical fencing is much easier to judge than Yumi's preferred classical style, with conductive circuits, recording equipment, and fast-shutter cameras to keep things accurate. A couple calls were overturned, but overall, it seemed pretty fair.

Wednesday morning is the epee qualifiers, and Yumi is so bored she almost goes to see if they'll take a late entry. Allory does well, of course, and ends up first seed in the impending double-elimination tournament. Samantha doesn't qualify, but then, Yumi didn't expect her too, and neither did Allory. None of her minions matter in the slightest to the Bitch Queen, and Yumi is pretty sure she forced Sam to join the team just to have someone to snark to and carry her bags. The saber round of thirty-two begins after lunch, and Yumi munches on her chocolate chip granola bar all alone in the stands until the giggling blondes get back from whatever slightly upscale chain they hit up for high-calorie baked goods.

"What, your little girlfriend isn't here to watch you get trounced?" Allory asks.

"You're looking a little extra tense today, Alls," Yumi says. "Did your massage not go well?"

Allory opens her mouth, then closes it again, teeth grinding. Honestly, it's probably for the best that Yumi got her treatment cancelled—otherwise, she might have missed open epee, and wouldn't *that* have been a shame?

Then Yumi catches the tail end of an announcement that makes the world seem to slow around her.

"Sun Teng," the speaker says. "Against Danielle Swain—"

"What's up, weirdo?" Allory asks. "You got something against Black people or something?"

Without realizing it, Yumi has been clutching her fists so tightly that her nails leave indentations in her palms. One even draws blood. She sees a dark figure down on the floor, one that looks up at her with yellow wolf eyes that contrast sharply with her dark skin.

She wasn't imagining things. It's her.

Danielle's outfit is black, in defiance of the guidelines of appropriate uniforms for the tournament. Black mask, black jersey, black knickers, black glove. Only her lamé is of a brighter color—red—as is the name "Swain" stenciled on the outside of her right leg. Danielle Swain makes it clear, from the first anyone sees her, that her matches will be different.

Her opponent, Sun Teng—who fences for Yale—steps onto the piste with a little wave to the crowd.

Danielle completely ignores the crowd and strides right to her place, shoves on her mask, and takes up her position without even saluting. There's an awkward pause while Sun salutes her, and Danielle belatedly waves her free hand dismissively, then assumes a fighting stance.

Yumi, watching in the stands, hears the wave of disapproving murmurs, and for good reason. This is highly irregular, skirting the edges of good taste and sportsmanship.

The judge checks both fencers are ready and shouts "fence!"

The first pass is over in two seconds, with Sun Teng on her butt on the piste, Danielle stands over her, saber raised for a killing blow. The judges are out of their seats, shouting "halt," and Danielle is already heading back to the on-guard line, saber held limply at her side and even dragging along the piste.

That show of contempt produces even more disgruntled murmurs, as well as a penalty assessed to Danielle. The judge looks very confident getting up to give it, but one glance at her face, and he seems to crumble. A touch is awarded to Sun, but when the judge sits back down, he looks about twenty years older.

For most people watching the bout, it must seem like Danielle is just light years better than poor Sun, but Yumi sees things differently. On the second pass, she feels the world slow when the judge shouts "fence!", and she sees Danielle move at normal speed while Sun struggles to start moving forward. Their powers activating together like this sets up a resonance that reverberates in Yumi's head enough to make her vaguely ill.

Once during a pass, Danielle turns her face slightly to look at Yumi, smiling cruelly, and that only makes the headache worse.

The rest of the bout only takes about ninety seconds. It doesn't even go past round one.

Afterward, with the score fifteen to one—the touch Danielle gave up for bad sportsmanship—as Sun stands trembling to maintain her composure in the face of being so brutally owned on the piste, Danielle turns to receive the officials' judgment. The crowd applauds awkwardly, but mostly people are shocked and unsure how to feel. Yumi knows how *Danielle* feels, though: smugly satisfied.

The two lock eyes from across the crowded arena, and it's like the world draws to a halt around them. People pause in mid-step on the stairs, a spilling soda sloshes out as eyes slowly go wide around it, and sound drags out and goes still. At least a hundred yards separate them, but they might as well be facing each other on a piste. Only now does Danielle salute, lifting her sword to point straight at Yumi's heart.

Yumi shivers, her whole body locking up as though Danielle actually stabbed her.

Her heart thunders in her head.

Muramasa sparks inside the fencing bag on the seat at her side, and she can feel its warmth against her leg. Smoke curls up from the zipped bag as the sword burns to life and practically wills itself into her open hand. And why not? She could call the sword to her hand, bound down the rows of spectators, and make an end of this right here, right now, in front of all these people. She almost does it, too, heaving and furious.

A confrontation with Danielle is coming, much as she might try to avoid it.

Then she sees Lisa apologizing her way down the row of seats toward her, and she abruptly shoves those feelings aside. She gasps for breath and only grabs her fencing bag at the last minute, wisps of smoke dissipating in the air. She crams the bag under her seat just a second before Lisa arrives, tray of two coffees in hand, and they one-arm hug in greeting.

"Hey!" Lisa sits down and shifts around, surprised. "Ooh, it's warm."

"Uh," Yumi says. "How was the spa treatment? You look great."

It's true, after all. Lisa looks gorgeous—a little bit flushed, her hair vibrant, her eyebrows plucked, all that. She's not even wearing much makeup: subtle touches of foundation and eyeshadow much lighter than the dark shades she tends to favor. But most importantly, her body language is relaxed, and she looks more natural and confident than Yumi has ever seen her.

"Thanks!" The old Lisa would probably have blushed and stuttered, but the newly relaxed and loosened up Lisa sighs contentedly. "It was a-*mazing*. Do you do that kind of thing all the time?"

"Not really. Why?"

Abruptly, a little of old Lisa reemerges, and she blushes. "I mean, uh, you look ... uh—"

"Moisturized?" Yumi asks with a little smile.

"Yes," Lisa says, relieved. "That's it."

Last night, Yumi got to witness Lisa go from awkward, retiring uncertainty to moaning, knee-trembling bliss under the capable hands of the Marriott's best masseuse, Toni. The woman had some major skills, and Yumi appreciated every cent of the expense. They both slept really well after that, leaving the TV on all night and sharing a bed like teen girls at a sleepover.

Well, except for the nightmare, but seeing Lisa today almost makes her forget about the Melting Woman.

It all seemed very natural and easy, which was good, because Yumi had been a bit nervous. She knew Lisa liked girls, and *she* liked girls, but she wasn't sure Lisa knew that, or how Lisa felt about her—what if she wasn't the *kind* of girl Lisa liked? How was she supposed to make a move? And after the massage and dinner, they were too relaxed and well-fed and comfortable to talk about it, let alone actually do anything. And in the morning, Lisa was up before her, busily typing on her tablet, coffee made, when Yumi stumbled into the walk-in shower.

"*Ohayo!*" Lisa had said by way of greeting, without looking up.

"Morning," Yumi had said back, confused.

Nothing about, y'know, sleeping together or anything.

Yumi has been thinking about that all morning, and she's reached no conclusions.

Why can't girls be easy, like boys? With boys, you know where you stand. There are even obvious, built-in visual aids. With girls, everything's way more ambiguous. Way more complicated.

Or maybe Yumi's just a doofus, and she's missing all the signs.

Muramasa simmers, warm and unsatisfied.

"Tall skinny soy latte. They didn't have coconut." Lisa hands over one of the coffees and takes a sip of her own. She sees Sun Teng heading toward the locker rooms, trying to hold back tears. "Is it over? What'd I miss?"

"Aside from Danielle Swain wiping the floor with her opponent's face, not much."

"Really?" Lisa frowns. "You said Teng was really good?"

"Yeah." Yumi looks out over the arena again, but Danielle has disappeared. Muramasa puts Yumi on the alert, ready for an attack, but she tries to suppress it. Danielle won't make a move on her in public—she would have done that already. What's her game?

Lisa scans her tablet. "Oh, I was looking forward to seeing Ariana Matthews from Northwestern. You should watch her, too—if she wins this match, which she probably will, you'll be fighting her tomorrow."

"Yeah?" Yumi expels a long, uneasy breath. "Ok."

~

Other than Danielle's brutal show, the rest of the third day of Nationals passes largely uneventfully, with some excellent skill and passion. All the semi-finals are on Friday, with the final bouts on Saturday. By Thursday afternoon, Yumi has won two more matches, landing her in the semi-finals.

Yumi would even enjoy it if not for the growing dread.

They're good fighters, the women who Yumi comes up against, but she ultimately beats them one way or another. Lindsay

Moorcock from Duke gives her a tough time in their quarter-finals bout, and Yumi gives up six touches in that bout, but ultimately she's just a speed bump on her way to the semi-finals. She's collected some buzz as she ascends through the ranks—the familial connection, and CCU's reputation, mostly—and eventually everyone is smiling at her and giving her encouraging gestures.

The biggest challenge—and the thing that's still making her uneasy—is managing her powers.

A lot of Yumi's power-set is automatic. It kicks in when she's in danger, and on the piste, that's basically all the time. She's gotten better at tuning it out, but there were a few times there where she felt ... She doesn't really know. Not like she's cheating, exactly, but it doesn't seem really fair. And by day four, it weighs on her.

How much time does she spend really fighting, as opposed to how much she spends putting on a show to hide the fact that she has powers? Trying to compensate for them makes her sloppy— reckless—apt to act without thinking, going by instinct and training rather than strategy. If anything, her powers are more of a hindrance than a benefit.

But she's the only one policing herself, so is that really fair?

Lisa, of course, couldn't be more thrilled by Yumi's success. The shyness has all but disappeared, and she even cheers and whoops during Yumi's quarter-finals match. The retiring wallflower Yumi met when they were freshmen would never be caught dead expressing that much enthusiasm at all, let alone in public. She's happy, and that makes Yumi happy too.

Not to mention they keep sleeping in the same bed, not that Yumi knows what *that* means.

Now it's just the semis, and then the finals. She always thought she had a good shot at winning this, and now she feels unstoppable.

Unstoppable, that is, except for Danielle Swain.

Danielle set an example with her first bout, and she continues to fight in the same style: brutal, efficient, and quick. She never expends a single ounce of energy she doesn't need to expend, and no one even touches her. Other than her periodic penalties for bad sportsmanship and the shows of contempt, it looks like she's going to have a near perfect score going into the finals.

And she's *definitely* going to the finals—no one seems to have a chance against her.

Or at least that's what it looked like ... until she came up against Allory Greene.

Allory acquitted herself well, despite over-extending herself to fight two weapons—epee in the morning, saber in the afternoon. By Thursday afternoon, she had already fought three times before her bout with Danielle. Yumi fully expected Danielle to breeze through that bout, but for some reason, Allory landed a touch on her. And another. And another.

The crowd cheered wildly for Allory—the righteous princess taking down the tournament's dastardly heel—but Yumi could only watch in disgust. She knew the truth: Danielle was throwing the fight. Sure, she made it look real, but Yumi knew her well enough to recognize the signs. And she knew why. She'd had Lisa double-check her math: if Danielle wanted to fight Yumi in the finals, she needed to come at her from the loser's bracket. She could have stayed in the winner's bracket, but then she would have come against Yumi in the semis, and that wouldn't be enough for Danielle.

This strategy also has two other consequences: it puts Allory solidly in Yumi's path, and it lets Danielle eliminate all the other fencers in the loser's bracket.

Just now, for instance.

Janine Marks, Yumi's opponent from Tuesday, has done really well in the competition, but she has the misfortune of coming up against Danielle in the quarter-finals late on Thursday, and Yumi can only suffer through watching her get absolutely *destroyed* in their match. It's not even close, and Danielle makes Janine look like a child with a stick, not a trained fencer with a saber. The bout lasts exactly sixteen passes, none of them longer than five seconds. About three minutes of fencing, and aside from almost hitting Danielle once by dumb luck, Janine looks like she's never picked up a saber.

The last pass, she tries her crazy flèche move, and Danielle drops into a stop-thrust, basically doing the splits, and Janine smashes into the point of her saber so hard it knocks her spinning to the ground. There's no question about any of the points—no questions of direct or indirect. Janine never even comes close to touching Danielle. Just qualifying for Nationals is an accomplishment, but getting stomped like that in her final bout must be utterly demoralizing.

Yumi can't help but feel for Janine, and when she finds her crying in the locker room afterward, she clenches her fists and jaw. Yumi opens and closes a locker, so Janine knows she's there before she appears, and she's glad she did. It gives Janine a chance to present herself the way she wants, which is with tears wiped away.

Not looking at each other directly, they strip off their outer gear in uneasy silence—the jackets hang open, the gloves come off, and so do the piste shoes. Yumi didn't shower and change after her quarter-finals match, but rather stayed to watch Janine take on Danielle, and that gives her plausible deniability for being here. It doesn't have to be awkward, though of course, the match that just happened ...

"Are you ok?" Yumi asks at length, though she knows the answer.

"I—" Janine sighs, long and deep. "I don't know what happened. I was just having a bad day, I guess."

"No." Yumi grits her teeth. "You fought great. Danielle Swain is just—"

"She just what?"

Yumi bites her tongue. She can't very well out someone for having powers. "Hey, you came in the top five nationally. You're one of the best fencers in the country. No one can take that away from you." She puts out her hand.

Janine looks at her hand dubiously. "You're going to the finals, right?"

"Maybe," Yumi says. "But probably. I just have to beat Allory tomorrow."

"That white bitch on your team?"

"That's the one."

"You stomp her good." Janine smiles. "And you beat Danielle Swain in the finals."

"I'll do my best."

They shake hands, and Yumi has extra purpose now.

"You need to shower?" Yumi asks. "I can wait."

"Nah, I'm just gonna crash. Good luck tomorrow."

"Thanks."

46

Janine leaves, and Yumi strips off the rest of her kit, wincing slightly. One of the touches got her right over her heart, and it was a big hit that she felt even through the chest protector. Gods above and beyond, the plastic is actually *cracked*. She got careless and rushed into an admittedly brilliant stop-thrust. She'll have to see about getting a new one.

Yumi turns on the shower and just lets the hot water flow over her, plastering her hair to her shoulders and halfway down her back. She touches the developing bruise on her chest. Lindsay really deserved that one, but it hurts like a *bitch*. Breathing in the steam, she massages the sore spot.

A locker clicks out in the locker room, but that's not so unusual, nor is it alarming. She left Muramasa safely locked away, and no one else could easily pick it up, anyway—not without burning themselves. No conversation, though, or any other cue. Yumi's not sure who else would be in the locker room.

"Hello?" she asks, but there's no reply. Maybe whoever it is just didn't hear her.

Or maybe it's something else, and not a person at all.

Maybe it's the Melting Woman.

Then one of the other showers turns on, and she sees, despite the heavy steam, a dark shape across the way. Yumi breathes a sign of relief—Janine must have changed her mind about that shower. She almost says something, but that'd be a little weird, wouldn't it? It's not like Yumi knows Janine all that well, and Janine didn't talk to her first, so she can respect the woman's privacy.

God, she's tired. The fighting itself isn't bad, but she's just emotionally drained. For three days, she's constantly worried about the ethics of even *being* in the tournament, let alone the exact way in which she can keep her powers hidden. She feels like she's back in a closet, the inside of which she hasn't seen since she was thirteen. Which was about when her powers started to manifest, too. Being a pansexual high schooler wasn't too hard when you could point to hot celebrities doing it, and growing up with wealth privilege in Seattle sure didn't hurt. The powers, though—those she kept secret, not out of some sort of duty, but because her mother asked her to. She knew, well enough, what could happen with unwanted scrutiny.

When Yumi was a kid, being a superhero seemed amazing, and you could publicly have powers and it would be no problem. The worst thing that would happen would be a scrap with old criminal rivals, and they'd end up in jail, at least until they broke out and the cycle repeated. But all the old teams were gone now—Agents of Awesome dissolved, the Protectorate broke up, the Supergroup tragedy—and her mother had the accident. By the time Yumi got to become a hero, it didn't seem all that fun anymore. And now, with that fascist Prather in office, cracking down on capes ...

Distracted, she reaches out to grab the soap, but she only succeeds in knocking it bouncing across the tile toward Janine.

"Shit," she says. "I'm sorry. Can you grab that for me? Just kick it back over?"

The figure pauses for a second, looking at Yumi through the steam. Then she turns off her water, stoops for the soap, and steps in her direction.

"Oh, I didn't mean you had to—" Yumi starts to say.

Then Danielle Swain appears, like an apparition out of fog, her yellow eyes cold and her lips curled in a non-smile.

The world slows around them, and Yumi can see the individual wisps of steam curling. But it's been so long since she let herself use her powers that when she staggers back, trying to get into a defensive position, she slips and ends up on her backside. She scuttles back against the wall, bracing herself for an attack.

"Heh," Danielle says. "Relax, Kujikawa. I have no intention of hurting you."

"Oh yeah?" Yumi climbs back to her feet. "So what do you want, Dani?"

"Ugh." Danielle makes a face. "Don't call me that."

"Ok, Dani."

The assassin rolls her eyes. "As for what I want, it's the same thing you want." She holds out the bar of soap. "A shower."

Yumi looks at the soap like it's a viper or a bomb.

"Oh, for fuck's sake." Danielle rolls her eyes again. "Grow up. I'm not going to kill you, and I'm not trying to see you naked."

Yumi realizes she's been instinctually covering herself, and she intentionally does away with that show of timidity. She snatches the proffered soap and stands proudly in front of Danielle.

48

"That's better." Danielle closes her hand and drops it back to her side. "You do look pretty good naked, by the way."

"Thanks," Yumi says. "You, uh, too."

That's an understatement. Danielle is a perfect physical specimen, with the robust build of an accomplished swordswoman, her muscles well-defined without being body-builder overt: functional strength, not aesthetic. Though Yumi could break her hand on those abs if she's not careful and those glutes, *wow*. Danielle's a little bit taller and longer than the classic *sabreur*, which befits a generalist. She is, after all, an international assassin; probably, she could kill someone with a toothpick, a nickel, or a bar of fucking soap.

Yumi tries not to be attracted to her and utterly fails, per usual.

"So, what school are you representing?" Yumi asks. "Do you even go to school?"

"Prather U," Danielle says. "I enrolled last week. Philosophy."

"Of course." A fraud college for a fraudulent entry.

"Is that really what you want to talk about?" Danielle asks. "You want me to wash your back?"

"Stop it." Yumi pointedly makes a show of using the soap, which she hopes doesn't contain poison or a bomb or anything. "I can't imagine the Factory actually cares about collegiate sports."

"More than you'd think, actually," Danielle says. "It's a great résumé builder. Signals respectability and instills confidence. National fencing champion, two-time gold medalist—"

"Drowned eight kittens in one bathtub," Yumi adds, then smirks. "Sorry, was that not current? I haven't checked your stats recently—maybe you're up to twelve."

"Always antagonize." Danielle shakes her head, refusing to take the bait. "You've made your contempt for my career path pretty clear."

"But you're still here to recruit me, right?" Yumi asks.

"These tournaments *are* good for scouting."

Figures. Danielle would have moved on her much earlier, but the Factory still wants her. Wants *Muramasa*, more like, but Yumi is the only one who can safely wield the sword. Plus, she's fought Danielle to a standstill once before. She's a good prospect, if they can turn her.

49

"Don't you think you'd have a little better luck if you were, I dunno, nicer to me?" Yumi intentionally turns her back to Danielle and washes off the soap. "Like, trying to convince me? Promising me lots of money, maybe? Heck, try seducing me, maybe? Isn't that something you spy types do?"

"Seducing you." Danielle speaks softly right in her ear. Her strong body touches Yumi's in a number of places. "You sure I'm not?"

Yumi takes a sharp breath. "Tease," she says, though the dismissal doesn't sound as firm as she intended. "You're gonna have to do better than that, straight girl."

"Hmm." Danielle moves in closer, pushing Yumi lightly against the wall. One dark hand appears around Yumi's chest and turns the water warmer, while another touches low on her belly. "Who said I'm straight?"

Oh *shit*. Yumi shivers all over, and she can feel Muramasa stir in response. She feels entirely too good. And very dangerous.

"I think you're bluffing," Yumi says, trying to sound defiant.

"Call."

Danielle's fingers creep lower.

"Uhh—"

Muramasa flares. The sword is still nearby, in the locker, waiting. And it's that heat that lets Yumi pull away, slipping out of Danielle's light hold and away into the steam. The sword appears in her hand, the fire banishing some of the moisture around her. She stands, half bent over, shoulders heaving, ready to pounce.

"What?" Danielle steps into Yumi's place and uses the water she just abandoned to scrub her face, looking quite innocuous. "Don't tell me you don't have needs."

"We, uh, we might be colleagues someday," Yumi says. "Maybe we should keep things professional."

"Maybe." Danielle turns to her, water dripping down her face and body in a very distracting way. "So you are considering it."

"I didn't say that," Yumi says, but it sounds weak. "Maybe you'll defect to my side."

That makes Danielle smirk slightly. Yeah, it didn't sound convincing to Yumi either.

"Aren't you tired of this?" Danielle shakes her head. "Of pretending?"

"Pretending what?"

"To be something you're not."

Danielle suddenly steps forward into Yumi's reach, heedless of the burning sword, and touches her wrist, holding the blade wide. Their eyes meet, and they stand there, lungs heaving.

"Let go," Danielle says. "Fear. Guilt. Remorse. Let go."

Yumi sucks in a breath.

Then she sees a figure behind Danielle—an amorphous but vaguely human-shaped visage—who stands amongst the steam and hot water. The Melting Woman's skin and flesh run and slough away, and she raises one hand to point an accusing finger in Yumi's direction.

Yumi pulls away from Danielle and drops back into a defensive stance. For just a second, Danielle looks over her shoulder, curious, but obviously she doesn't see anything.

"You're not ready. You still think these things matter. But you will learn. You will join us eventually."

"What—" Yumi pants, chest heaving. "What makes you so sure?"

"Because this is who you are. Unfettered, unrestrained, un .. closeted."

With that, Danielle walks away through the steam.

Yumi stands alone in the shower for a moment. In her hand, Muramasa blazes hot, making the steam evaporate around it. She's almost cleared out the shower, and she realizes belatedly that it's a public place, and someone might see her holding a fiery sword. That'll raise some questions she doesn't have good answers for. She should hide it in the relative safety of her locker—but she just stands there staring at it.

Danielle is absolutely right. Why should she have to pretend? Can't she just...?

"Fuck."

Voices out in the locker room draw her attention, and she perks up like a hunted animal. She tosses Muramasa back into the corner of the showers, where a little steam is still lingering, and heads toward the lockers. Sure enough, several fencers from elsewhere in the competition have come in, comparing notes about upcoming matches.

They aren't the ones who concern her, though. In the near row of lockers, next to Yumi's own designated locker, she sees Allory Greene casually brushing her hair and touching up her makeup with the aid of a compact, smiling smugly to herself. By the looks of things, she's been there for at least a few minutes.

Well, shit. How much did she hear?

Better get this over with.

With a sigh, Yumi grabs her towel to wrap around herself, then heads over toward the locker set aside for her use. Allory doesn't obviously react, but Yumi can tell she's using the compact to watch her. She pointedly opens the locker door to block her view, and changes with the view obscured.

At least she's got her underwear and her track pants on before Allory finally speaks up. "I was just kidding about the carpet-munching," she says. "I didn't realize you really *were* a dyke. I feel all homophobic now."

"Grow up."

Yumi intentionally doesn't look at her as she shoves her arms through the sleeves of her baggy CCU sweatshirt. It still smells like Mark, and while normally she likes that, right now it feels gross. She takes it back off and settles on just the tank top. She can deal with a little cold.

Most importantly, she holds Muramasa's scabbard in one hand above the other, then summons Muramasa into her hand inside the locker, where Allory can't see it, and right into the scabbard. It's a trick she's been working on, and she's pleased to see it work this time. The sword has quieted down to faint wisps of smoke leaking around the scabbard. She zips it into her bag, stuffed in the locker, and pulls the whole thing out. One good thing about traveling light, your bag can fit in a lot of safe places.

"A little nervous, huh, Kujikawa?" Allory asks. "Worried your secret's out?"

"That I'm pansexual?" Yumi slams the locker closed. "It's 2018, Allory. Grow up."

"Obviously *I* don't care." Allory snaps the compact closed and stands. "But do you think the Olympic committee's going to be so understanding?"

Yumi resists the urge to punch her, and instead just locks the locker. She pointedly doesn't look up at Allory, standing basically right there, or at Samantha giggling at the end of the row of lockers.

"Maybe I should ask Lisa about it," Allory says. "I wonder if CCU has rules about sleeping with the team manager—"

Now that. *That* Yumi isn't going to tolerate.

She leans in suddenly and slams one hand against the locker next to Allory's face, moving so fast and accurately it startles the other girl. Her eyes widen and her words cut off.

"Leave her alone," Yumi says. "This thing, whatever it is—it's between you and me. Got it?"

Allory stares at her, chest heaving. She licks her lips, about to speak.

Yumi is suddenly less certain she knows what's going on.

"Fine," Allory says at length. She looks away, a little ashamed. "It was just a joke."

"Ok." Yumi feels unsure, but she draws away after a second. "Just—let's just get this finished, ok? We both want to be here. Let's focus on fencing, ok?"

Allory doesn't say anything, and Yumi hefts her bag over her shoulder. She just took a shower, but now she wants another one, to clean off the white trash. Back at her room, where she doesn't run the risk of seeing any of these assholes. And sleep, *Jesus.*

She's about to flounce out when Allory speaks up again. "It was me, you know."

Yumi freezes in place and looks over her shoulder. "What did you say?"

"The Flasher story the other day. You know the one." Allory grins, her teeth entirely too white. "I'm the one who tipped them."

"What." Yumi looks at her. "What—what are you talking about?"

"Your powers, obvs," she says. "And how they're going to get you disqualified."

"Wait, what? Who told you I have powers?"

"What, other than you, just now?" Allory looks profoundly smug, which is her default look. "I've known it since last year, you stupid cow. A ninja girl just happens to show up in Cobalt City the same weekend you enroll at CCU? If you're trying to be subtle, that's really sad."

Shit. When Yumi worried about underestimating Allory, it never occurred to her that it might be her *brain* she'd underestimate.

"It wasn't that big a deal back at first," Allory says. "But then you just kept beating me, and I can't have that. Not in *Prather's* America."

"You probably voted for that bastard," Yumi says under her breath, almost a growl.

"So did your dad," Allory says. "He has money, doesn't he? Tell me—does he know about you?"

Shit shit shit. She's not just threatening to get Yumi disqualified from Nationals—if she gets outed, Prather's goons could come arrest her. They'd make an example of her, especially if they figure out her secret identity. And then her friends—the rest of Justice or Something. Father's connections can probably get her out of it, but what about Arnold? Friday? Prather *absolutely* hates people with any ties to Mexico.

Yumi feels sick. "What ... what do you want?"

Allory grins evilly. "You throw the match tomorrow," she says, "or I'll post a follow-up you really won't like. Make sure my friends at the DHS and the DSHA get tagged, too."

"You mean your *daddy's* friends."

"Keep talking, rich girl," Allory says. "I'm sick of your liberal superiority. You're a fraud, and I can prove it." Her thumb hovers over her phone. "Maybe I'll just post it right now."

Yumi hesitates, and Allory smiles. She slips her phone into her bra.

"I know you'll make the right decision," she says.

CHAPTER 5

The overhead lights in the presidential suite living room are a little too bright for Lisa's headache, so they've settled on a bunch of candles Yumi had the front desk send up. She didn't consciously intend it to be as romantic as it feels, but if Lisa notices, she doesn't say anything. She's absorbed in her tablet, looking at the upcoming matches.

"You're doing really well," she says. "You and this Danielle Swain are definitely going to be in the finals. I didn't know Prather U had a fencing team—"

Yumi, pacing around the room, sighs. She's restless, unable to focus on anything in particular. Danielle's offer and their confrontation in the shower. Allory's threat. The Melting Woman ...

"I don't know," she says. "I mean, yeah, she's the best, but—"

"You're *both* the best," Lisa says. "I've watched your bouts. You're fencing better than you ever did at CCU. If anyone can beat her, it's you."

"Maybe."

They lapse into silence again, with Lisa tapping in a few more commands—studying videos, probably, or crunching the numbers. She's a poli-sci major, but she's one of those weird ones who takes math and science seriously as electives, and she's in advanced calculus. At this rate, she's going to graduate with at least a double-minor before she goes to law school. Way more focused than Yumi, who started out in Anthropology but as of year two is looking for a new major.

"Well, you know about Miyamoto Musashi, of course," Lisa says at length.

"What?" Yumi turns to find Lisa holding up a picture on her tablet of a classic samurai woodcut.

"The sword-saint of Japan, who wrote the Five Rings?" Lisa rolls her eyes. "He fought over sixty duels, entirely undefeated. One of his most famous was with Sasaki Kojiro, another prominent swordsman, who everyone thought was undefeatable."

"So two masters," Yumi says. "Like Danielle and me."

"Right," Lisa says. "They fought on the island of Funajima. Kojiro arrived early, with all his allies and supporters, but Musashi came late. When he finally arrived on the late tide, Kojiro and his people were exhausted and frustrated with the wait. Musashi hadn't even brought a sword, either. He had to spend a long time carving a bokken from one of his oars and used that, which only made Kojiro more frustrated. When they finally faced each other, Musashi positioned himself so that when he dodged, the sun would be in Kojiro's eyes. He killed Kojiro with a single blow, then fled the island before his angry supporters could take revenge."

"So I'm Musashi in this story?" Yumi asks. "And you're saying I need to use tricks to win?"

"No, you're Kojiro," Lisa says. "You keep expecting Danielle to fight fair, and the more you watch her being disrespectful and dishonorable, the more you feel justified in defeating her. The more *right* you are—that it'd be cosmically unfair for anything else to happen. And when you face her, that'll be a weakness. She'll win, because she's in your head."

"Oh." Yumi nods. "I didn't know you read Japanese history."

"Not really," Lisa says. "But I read a lot of manga and watch a lot of anime, and it's a popular story. There's this whole scene in *Full Metal—*"

"That makes more sense."

"Hey!" Lisa says in mock offense.

But Yumi isn't in the mood to banter. She blows out a sigh and slumps over the arm of the couch, raven hair with red tips spread out around her head, feet dangling off the end.

"I might not even fight her, you know," Yumi says.

"What? Of course you will."

"I have to beat Allory tomorrow."

"What, are you serious?" Lisa scoffs. "It's Allory. You always beat her."

"She beat Swain."

"Swain lost that fight on purpose, and we both know it," Lisa says. "There's no way you'll lose to Allory. She doesn't even fence saber because—" Her eyes widen. "You *are* serious. Why?"

"Um—" Yumi almost tells her the truth—about Allory blackmailing her—but she can't. There's too much to explain, and she's just too tired to go into all of it. Plus, if Lisa knows she was lying to her all this time ... She shuts her eyes. "Weren't you just telling me not to be overconfident?"

"That's not—" Lisa sighs. "Move over."

Yumi sits up, her expression quizzical, while Lisa sits on the couch near her head. Yumi makes to adjust, but Lisa pats her thighs in an inviting way. They share a wordless acknowledgement, and then Yumi settles back down, head in Lisa's lap.

"What's wrong?" Lisa asks, running strands of Yumi's hair between her fingers.

"I—" Yumi sighs. "I don't know. It's just ... this all seemed so simple when we got here. I've been training for this my whole life. Living up to my mother's example. Working toward the Olympics." She closes her eyes. "But now, I'm just not sure."

"So what do *you* want?" Lisa asks.

"I don't know."

Damn, she's comfy. Lisa's lap is warm and soothing. She doesn't ask Yumi any more questions but keeps running her fingers through her hair and occasionally touching her forehead. It's really nice, and Yumi feels like she can relax for the first time in days.

"You know, maybe you *could* be Musashi."

"How do you mean?"

"Maybe it's time to get in *her* head a little."

Yumi shifts to let Lisa up, and she heads toward the bathroom, where a whole bag of beauty accessories sits waiting next to the sink—compliments of the front desk. Apparently, Lisa might have dropped a hint or two during her treatment, and Toni the massage therapist made sure the items got delivered. Yumi sees her sit on the edge of the bath and turn the faucet, and steaming water thunders from the tap.

"What are you doing?" Yumi asks, getting up.

"Come on," Lisa says.

Yumi heads into the bathroom, where Lisa is pouring a generous amount of bubble bath into the tub. "You're taking a bath?"

"You are," Lisa says. "Come on, you're super tense. You need to relax your muscles. Didn't you take a big hit today?"

"Ok, but—" Yumi's hands pause at her belt clasp.

Red points light on Lisa's cheeks, and she turns her back. "Don't worry, that's what the bubbles are for."

"Ok."

Yumi disrobes, acutely aware of her body as she does. Lisa's right—her muscles feel tense, and without her clothes, she feels both vulnerable and tired. Out of the corner of her eye, she sees Lisa's face in the mirror, but she's got one hand over her eyes just to make sure she preserves Yumi's privacy. For some reason, that strikes Yumi as profoundly funny, and she stifles a giggle as she slips into the tub. The warm water feels great, enveloping her in a gentle embrace, and the bubbles give it an extra level of comfort.

"Ok." Yumi takes a handful of bubbles and blows it. "I'm in."

"Ok." Lisa peeks out between her fingers, then turns to look at Yumi in the tub. "Right."

"What now?" Yumi asks.

Lisa goes to the bag on the counter and rummages for a second before she produces a box of what looks like hair dye. She scans the cover, looks at Yumi's very dark hair with red streaks, and nods.

"Seriously?" Yumi asks. "You're going to dye my hair? Right now?"

"Absolutely." Lisa breaks the seal on the lightener tube, then slows her roll. "I mean, unless you don't want me—"

"No—I mean, I'm down," she says. "But, I mean, won't that take all night?"

"Uh uh," she says. "Normally, yes, we'd have to do lightener on most of your hair, wait forty minutes, lightener on your roots, wait even longer, *then* do the color—you'd be in the salon all day. But this—this is *Trans-Mane*. It can turn any color hair into any other color, depending on what you want, and it only takes about an hour." She shows Yumi the box, which features a gender ambiguous person with swirling hair that becomes different colors depending on the angle. "It was invented by Dr. Synthia Corbin, formerly the superhero Big Head, formerly of Supergroup—" She stops short of deadnaming the super genius hero, obviously.

"Oh yeah," Yumi says. "I've heard of that. It's top of the line stuff. How'd you afford that?"

Lisa bites her lip. "Uh, I put it on the room."

"Seems legit." Yumi grins.

Lisa inspects the hairbrush, which has a little control pad built into it. "This was what I had in mind," she says, showing Yumi the read-out.

"Oh." Yumi feels warm inside. "Totally."

"Cool." Lisa programs the dye, and it takes on a particular sheen within the transparent plastic tube. "That should do it."

Yumi scrutinizes her. "Are you sure you know how to do this?"

"Who do you think dyes *my* hair?" Lisa asks, brushing some green strands back out of her face.

"You do it yourself?" Yumi nods, impressed. "I thought you went to a salon or something."

"I mean, I don't use Trans-Mane. I'm a starving college student. But don't worry, I'm basically a professional." Lisa snaps the gloves on, then winces and rubs at her wrist. "Ow."

Yumi giggles. "Are we really doing this?"

"Absolutely." Lisa picks up the dye tube and holds it casually and confidently. "Lie back."

"Ok."

She does as instructed, and Lisa sits down on the edge of the tub, extremely close to Yumi's face. After arranging Yumi's hair into quadrants on a plastic sheet, and that on top of one of the fluffy hotel towels, she gets to work. Lisa essentially paints the dye on, which makes Yumi giggle a little at the faint tugging, but Lisa seems very serious. She's making art.

The actual process of applying the dye is pretty fast, but it's at that point that Lisa starts working it in with her fingers. She's very thorough, rubbing the dye into every bit of Yumi's hair. That alone feels nice, but when she gets to Yumi's scalp, the massage feels like heaven. She sighs, closes her eyes, and loses herself in the little sensations. Lisa's fingers make her whole body shiver.

In the other room, Muramasa flickers to life where Yumi stashed it behind the couch, but she's only dimly aware of it.

The only sounds are the periodic drips of water from the faucet, the soft sizzle of bubbles evaporating, the faint thwish-thwish of Lisa working the dye into Yumi's hair.

"There," Lisa says at length. "Now we've got to wait while that sets."

Like waking from a dream, Yumi opens her eyes again, to see Lisa's face hovering close to her own, inspecting her handiwork.

"I think I caught most of the dye with one of the towels—I didn't get much on the tile," she says. "The towel is totes ruined, though."

Totes. Yumi can't help but smile. Lisa may be a reserved Japanese maiden, but she's also a California girl. "Don't worry, we'll just steal it," she says.

That makes Lisa smile. She wraps up Yumi's hair in the towel. Yumi sits, unmoving and cooperative, while Lisa gets the few errant strands sticking to her neck and bare shoulders. Lisa is definitely sneaking glances at her face, though.

"What?" Yumi asks at length.

"Oh, uh," Lisa says. "Just, your eyes are really beautiful. I don't know if I ever told you that."

"You did," Yumi says. "The first time we met. At the CCU bookstore."

"I did?"

"Though the word you used was *pretty*."

"Oh." Lisa blushes. "Right. That was, like, really embarrassing."

"It was adorable, you mean," Yumi says. "My hair was blue, and you said I looked like Rei."

Lisa brightens. "You're so not like Rei," she says. "I'm more like Rei."

"Because you're an emotionless clone?" Yumi asks. "Or because your dorm room is full of underwear and like, one pair of glasses?"

"You know what I mean," Lisa says. "You're more of a Misato."

"Hey," Yumi says. "I'm at *least* an Asuka."

"You *wish* you were an Asuka."

Yumi likes the way Lisa is looking down at her: warmly and openly, without judgment. Mark never looked at her that way, even before the Melting Woman came between them. Lisa doesn't know

60

everything about Yumi, but she knows a lot. Surely it's ok to tell her the truth. To talk to her about this.

"Listen, Lisa——" she says.

The warmth evaporates from Lisa's expression, and she puts her shields back up immediately. "You—you don't have to say it," she says, pausing. "I'm sorry."

"Say what?" Yumi asks, suddenly bewildered. "Did I say something wrong?"

"No, I——" Lisa goes back to massaging the dye into Yumi's hair, as if focusing on work will distract her. "It's my fault. I was stupid. We're just friends, and——"

"Wait, hold on." Yumi reaches up and touches her wrist. Their eyes meet. "What do you mean? I mean, we *are* friends, but——"

"But?" Lisa says softly, her lip quivering. "I'm sorry, I——"

"But I really want to kiss you," Yumi says.

"You ... you do?"

"Yes."

"Oh." Lisa's cheeks flush. "Ok."

"Ok?"

"Yes."

Yumi leans up, hair dripping with dye, and kisses Lisa. She tenses up, but it must only be because she's startled, because then she's kissing Yumi back with surprising energy and passion. Released tension flows through Yumi, and her whole body lights up with tingles. Their tongues connect and a shudder passes through Lisa, as though she's been wanting to do that for a long time, too.

At length, Lisa pulls away, leaving Yumi half-submerged in the bath, lips still pursed.

"Wow." Lisa touches her lips, leaving a little streak of dye on her skin. "That ... I——"

"I really like you, Lisa," Yumi says. "Plus, do you have *any* idea how good that feels?"

"Yes?" Lisa smiles shakily and flexes her gloved fingers. "It's the way they did in my treatment yesterday. I picked up a new technique. Did I do ok?"

"Um, *yes.*"

"Oh. Ok."

Lisa looks dreamy, as though she's trying to wake up from a fantasy, but when she sees Yumi climbing out of the tub, her cheeks go red, and she turns away. She takes off the plastic gloves and tosses them toward the trash bin. She misses, of course.

"I—I thought you liked boys," Lisa says. "I mean, you have a boyfriend—"

"What? Who told you that?"

"Um."

Lisa stoops down to pick up the dye-stained gloves, but of course they've left some dye on the tile floor, so she has to grab a roll of toilet paper to clean it. She spins it several times before Yumi walks over and pulls it off the dispenser entirely.

"Thanks," Lisa says, still averting her gaze. "Aren't you and Mark Obiyashi dating?"

"No." Yumi wraps her arms around herself. It's chilly outside the bath, but until now, she hasn't felt it. "I mean, we did, but we broke up."

"Oh." Lisa wipes at the dye. "And you want me? *Me.*"

"Yes?"

Now it's Yumi's turn to frown. She lays her hands on Lisa's shoulders as she kneels there, making her stiffen, then relax. She draws Lisa to her feet, though she's still not facing her. Yumi caresses her arms and shoulders.

"Why wouldn't I want you?"

"I'm ... I'm just *me*," she says. "I'm not beautiful, or rich, or glamorous. Just—"

One bare arm wrapped around Lisa, Yumi presses her bath-slick body against her back, and Lisa relaxes back into her with a deep sigh. She turns her head halfway, and Yumi presses her lips to her neck.

"I'm just me," she says, but it isn't a protest. It's more of a question, and Yumi answers it.

"Yes."

Lisa turns to face her, and then they're kissing again. This time, they're pressed together, face to face, hands wandering over their bodies. Once she's past Lisa's outward reserve, Yumi finds a hot, passionate woman, and it fills her with rising excitement that banishes any concerns about the cold. They make their slippery, messy way across the massive bathroom and end up back in the

62

bathtub. Lisa climbs in, clothes and all, and immediately they pull apart, laughing like madwomen.

Yumi helps Lisa out of her wet clothes, enjoying the whole process, and then they're in the bath together, kissing and caressing and ...

"Wait," Yumi says. "Is that—smoke?"

They both scramble out of the bath as the fire alarm starts to ring.

Dripping, Yumi rushes into the main room, where the couch is smoldering. She knows immediately what happened, because Muramasa is burning in her mind's eye. She extends a hand without even thinking, but Lisa comes into the room, wrapped in a towel and toting a fire extinguisher, and if she were to see Yumi just holding a flaming katana, she'd definitely have questions. Instead, she seems to think Yumi's pointing at the source of the burning, and she turns that way. With practiced efficiency, she pulls the pin on the extinguisher and sprays the heck out of the couch.

At just that moment, Yumi summons Muramasa, which appears in her hand at her call. The blade is glowing bright red with heat, leaking smoke and flames, and she immediately exerts her will over it, just as Sensei taught her. In the space of three seconds, the fire dims, and it becomes just a sword.

Without the source, the fire is out almost immediately.

"What happened?" Lisa asks. "Did a candle fall over?"

"Um." Yumi looks down at the sword, then whips it behind her back as Lisa turns toward her. "I don't know."

"Uh." Lisa stares at Yumi's bubble-bath covered body. "I, uh—"

"Um, how did you know how to do that?" Yumi asks. "With the extinguisher?"

"Oh, uh, Girl Scouts," Lisa says. "I should make sure I got it all. Um—"

"I'll get a robe."

Yumi hurries back into the bathroom and grabs one of the robes, which also gives her a chance to stash the troublesome ancestral katana in the tall closet next to the ironing board.

"Stay," she says under her breath. "And don't screw this up for me."

The katana, if it understands the command, offers no reply. It is, after all, just a sword.

When she gets back out to the living room, Lisa is on the phone with the front desk, assuring them that it was just a candle that set off the alarm. There doesn't seem to be any damage other than the burned couch.

Finally, Lisa hangs up the phone with a sigh. "Well, that happened."

"It's fine," Yumi says. "You think we're the first guests to burn a piece of furniture?"

"I still feel bad," Lisa says. "I should have put out the candles first—"

"No, it's my fault," Yumi says.

"You think?" Lisa asks. "I mean—"

"Definitely me."

Yumi lays a hand on Lisa's bare forearm, and their eyes meet. The momentary crisis fades away, and they both burn with the same sort of hunger as before.

"So—" Yumi smiles. "Where were we?"

"I think ... maybe there?" Lisa points to the bedroom.

"Seems legit."

~

Later, as they're lying in bed together, the fourth episode of a cooking competition show droning in the background, they take turns blinking and smiling at each other. This time, they're cuddled up facing each other, and Yumi's not sure she's ever fit with another body quite as well.

"So ... are we dating now?" Lisa asks.

"I hope so," Yumi says.

"That's a relief." Lisa blows out a sigh. "You kept making all these grand gestures, which might have been romantic, or maybe not. I thought if one more day went by—"

"I know, right?" Yumi asks. "We're too cute."

"Disgustingly cute."

Lisa adjusts her position, snuggling in closer until her face is up against Yumi's neck. "Have you, you know—?"

"What?" Yumi asks.

"I know you dated Mark," she says. "And I'm assuming other guys—"

"Hold up." Yumi half sits up in bed. "Are you asking if I've been with a woman before?"

"Well—"

Panic lights inside Yumi. She's been with a couple women before, but they were just teenagers trying to figure each other out. It's not like there was a readily available course on sapphic sex. "Was it, um, was it not good?"

"No, that's—" Lisa's face is ashen. "I've just, never—"

"Oh." Yumi's eyes widen. "Never? You mean, you're, uh ... not even with, you know, the hot Russian girl? With the undercut?"

"Svetlana? Lisa asks. "I mean, we've kissed a few times."

"Oh." Yumi has to admit, Lisa's pretty talented for never having done this before. "I just assumed, if you went to the Little Dutchgirl together—"

Lisa looks adorably confused. "Yeah, I never got that."

"Oh, it's like, the water is rising, and there's only one way to plug the dyke—"

"Oh. *Oh*." Lisa blushes furiously. "Hey, wait, how did you know about—?"

With a grin, Yumi kisses her again, and eventually the question drifts away, forgotten.

"Hey," Lisa says. "I don't suppose you could—"

"I sure can," Yumi says.

"Mmm."

Yumi does as requested, and Lisa breathes sharply, then moans.

"'Have you ever been with a woman before?'," Yumi murmurs. "*Honestly*."

"What?" Lisa starts to ask, then gasps.

Eventually, they fall asleep, and if Yumi has dreams that night, she doesn't remember them.

CHAPTER 6

The afternoon of the second to last day, Yumi squares off with Allory Greene in the semi-finals.

A bout between two fencers from the same club has a certain extra cachet to it. The expectation is that they know each other really well, so the bout might be the kind of choreographed masterpiece you see in movies. Either that, or the relationship between the two fencers gives it extra pathos, whether they're friends or, especially, if they're rivals. That's definitely the case with Yumi and Allory, as should be obvious to anyone who sees them take their positions on the piste. Allory makes a big production out of getting ready, making a ritual of tying her blonde hair back in pigtails, then putting on her pink-trimmed fencing jacket and mask, all to drum up support from the crowd with her show. Yumi, for her part, just does some stretches and some quick high knees to make sure she's limbered up. When she hits the floor, she already has her mask on.

The crowd has swelled in the last few days, the beneficiary of Allory's marketing efforts. As big as Allory's personality and presentation are, Yumi knows a lot of those eyes are on her. Allory's viral tweet didn't mention her by name, but there was enough info there to connect the dots. They're watching Yumi for signs of powers. Allory wants the biggest stage possible for her triumphant moment against Yumi.

Finally, they officially announce the combatants.

"Allory Greene, captain of the team from Cobalt City University, home of Stardust and the Protectorate," the person on the PA system says. "Also, uh, she's pre-med and—do I have to read this? Ok." Papers shuffle. "Announcing she's recently been accepted for Beach Girl Bachelorette 2018 this summer! Allory Greene."

Most of the audience applauds politely, except for a bunch of people in red Prather hats, who burst into obnoxious whoops, screams, and wolf-whistles. The alt-right cheering section seem to be following Allory around to her matches, and why not? She's the classic all-American, white, girl-next-door type, with her Valley Girl drawl, long blonde hair, and big blue eyes, like a young Candace Calloway, Prather's popular press secretary. Privately and not charitably, Yumi suspects the pre-med thing is just to make her sound compassionate, and she's really looking for a career on Faux News or as a right-wing Twitter celebrity. Of course, Allory eats up all the applause, blowing kisses to her devoted fans, all of them misogynists who wouldn't think twice about harassing or assaulting her if they thought they could get away with it. It makes Yumi more than a little sick.

When the announcer names her, she barely even hears him over all the noise. She reaches up and pulls off her mask, sweeping out her long hair, dyed a brilliant silver that catches the lights trained on the piste. The room goes utterly silent but for a collective gasp for air, and the world seems to slow around her as she shakes her head to free up the hair. The dye job isn't perfect—hard to get perfect with a home kit—but it's striking enough to make a statement. Yumi opens her eyes, revealing her red eyes to the cameras and thus the crowd. No colored contacts today to cover up the peculiar eye color she shares with her mother. The message is clear. The daughter of Kujikawa Eiko has embraced her legacy and returned to reclaim her title.

The arena is silent but for the faint click of camera phones and discharge of flashes as journalists snap pictures. The people seem to expect something, but Yumi has nothing to say. She salutes the crowd with her saber, turning it with a distinctive flourish, and looks down at the mat.

Then someone starts clapping wildly—Lisa, her hands stained with spots of silver dye—and the applause catches and spreads like wildfire. The roar of the crowd drowns out the red hats, some of whom clap grudgingly. Looking down, Yumi permits herself a small, private smile, crosses one leg behind herself, and bows deeply, sword out wide. She draws in the audience's applause, then rises again.

She and Allory face each other as the judge announces the bout. Allory's expression is neutral but her eyes are furious. "Going out with a big show, huh?" she asks through gritted teeth and a fake smile. "You didn't forget our conversation, right?"

Yumi smiles wolfishly. "Bring it, bitch."

Whatever Allory expected, it wasn't that, and she returns a look of pure hatred, one that looks a little intimidated. Good. Yumi is still smiling as she reaches back to secure her hair with a rainbow scrunchie she borrowed from Lisa that morning.

They take their places and salute, only a few paces of piste separating them. It's a decent distance, but Yumi knows how quickly an aggressive fencer can cover it, particularly one who hates her as much as Allory Greene does.

And when the judge says "fence!", that's exactly what Yumi gets: Allory comes rushing at her, crossing her feet in her haste to close. The judge immediately calls "halt," and Allory is penalized a touch for crossing her feet. That's fine in epee, but it's against the rules in saber. Allory loudly protests, throwing her arms wide, and that gets her a second penalty.

Yumi smiles at Allory through her mask. She can't throw the bout if Allory defeats herself.

This time when the judge says "fence," Allory gets control of herself. The world starts to slow in preparation, but Yumi doesn't need her powers to take Allory down. She picks the moment and stalks forward, low to the ground and taking full advantage of her superior form and lower center of gravity. Allory slashes down at her, but Yumi dives past and around her, dragging her saber along Allory's hip, just at the lower limit of the scoring area. It's a risky move, because Allory has the right of way, but Yumi attacks so fast, so unexpectedly, and inside her reach, that Allory can only flail at her, missing by about four inches. Yumi ends up slightly behind her, one knee bent, the other leg out behind her, saber wide, her outside foot just inside the border of the piste. She never crossed her feet.

"That one's for you, Janine," she whispers.

The audience erupts in applause and cheers, but Yumi barely hears them. She focuses on Allory spitting and sputtering in confusion.

"Ladies?" the judge asks. "On guard?"

They return to their starting positions, Yumi with a spring in her step, Allory fuming.

Allory is more cautious now, focusing on her form and balance. That she hasn't let the score rattle her is a testament to her discipline and talent—she's really a very good fencer, with a clear reach advantage thanks to being four inches taller—but there's no stopping Yumi now. She shifts her weight back and forth, stretching rather than taking up a defensive posture, and waits for Allory. She looks absolutely unconcerned. There are a few snickers from the audience and a few isolated claps, though the competitors-turned-spectators amongst them quickly shush that business.

When Allory gets within range, she feints and, in classic Allory fashion, goes for the coupe, whipping her saber over Yumi's blade to score a hit on her arm, probably. Yumi starts to parry, as though she's falling for the feint, but as soon as Allory twists her saber out of line, Yumi drops in the same fluid motion, compressing through the legs, and thrusts straight ahead to spit Allory right in the stomach, her saber bending slightly. It looks more like a foil move: if these were real swords, that'd be a mortal blow right there.

Sure enough, Allory's sword swings down and slaps her arm, but a split-second too late. The sensors go off, and Yumi gets the point—a clear right of way judgment. That's the danger of the coupe—it cedes right of way and is a surefire loser if a defender knows it's coming and has the grit to respond.

They should return to on guard, but Allory lingers a second to stare daggers down at Yumi.

"The fuck, Kujikawa?" she asks. "What are you doing?"

"Careful, Alls," Yumi says. "You *do* know how to fence, right?"

"I touched you that time, bitch," Allory says.

"Now you're just embarrassing yourself."

It's not the way Yumi likes to win—she doesn't like to be hit at all—but the goal here isn't just to win. It's to give Allory a taste of her own medicine: put her on the biggest fencing stage available, give her all the attention she craves, and let her make an utter fool of herself.

The next few passes don't lead to any touches, as Yumi eludes Allory's strikes and instead parries, ripostes, and keeps her at bay. Yumi keeps retreating toward her end of the piste, giving Allory virtually all the room, but the woman just can't hit her. Allory keeps ducking back away from Yumi's warding ripostes, and by the time she's ready to launch a major assault, the buzzer sounds, and the judges declare the end of round one.

Between the rounds, Lisa cheers for Yumi, jumping up and down and holding her glasses on with one hand. As serious as the bout is, Yumi has to smile at that.

"Have fun with it," Lisa told her before they headed to the piste, then kissed her.

Fun. Yumi can do fun.

In round two, Allory doesn't advance, but instead lets Yumi come to her. Yumi obliges, as she knows the judges won't tolerate no one moving, but she takes her time with it. She heads down the piste, bobbing up and down, three paces forward, two back, adjusting the angle of her saber from a high to low guard, peering along its length. She looks like a first-year fencer, utterly unsure of herself, but in light of the previous passes, the mockery is clear. Her antics draw a little more laughter from the audience. Finally, fed up with waiting, Allory presses forward and lunges, but Yumi steps into the attack, parries her saber, and slashes with a quick flick of her wrist across Allory's faceplate. Allory jerks back, stung, but the sensor has already gone off.

"Touch!" the judge announces. "Kujikawa."

Halfway through round two, with the score ten to zero in Yumi's favor, Allory is clearly frustrated. She came expecting an easy bout with an opponent who would throw the match. Sure, maybe Yumi would put on a good show, but it would basically be pretend fencing. This was supposed to be Allory's moment that would put her in the finals. Instead, Yumi is not only winning, but making Allory look like a novice on the piste. Her strong discipline fractures, and when the judges shout "fence!" for the fifth time in round two, Allory comes down the piste like a woman possessed. They meet in the middle, where Allory's saber, held in a high hanging guard, slashes down quick and heavy, but she's fast enough to lean back out of Yumi's range before a riposte can strike her.

This is, honestly, the best fencing she's done the whole tournament, and it shows.

Allory wins the next two touches. The first is a poorly set defense, and Allory tags Yumi's wrist with her saber after an exchange where they almost clash guards. The second is a messy exchange, where Allory disengages and eludes a prime parry to slap Yumi's arm hard enough to leave a faint bruise, setting the sensor off. Both good touches no one can challenge. At the end of the day, she does have the talent, and Yumi must concede that she deserves to be here on that basis.

Yumi gives ground, backing up half a step with each of Allory's strikes. They fence back and forth, blades clashing with echoing ringing noises, their bodies flexing forward and backward. The rhythm spins around the beating of Yumi's heart—now slower, now faster, neither of them able to break through.

Yumi chances a look over at the stands, and what she sees there makes the world slow around her, though she's trying not to use her powers. Lisa's still there, her shy countenance transformed by excitement and enthusiasm, holding up one fist in solidarity. Behind her, unseen, stands Danielle Swain. She's not wearing athletic clothes or fencing attire but just street clothes, including a dark gray hoodie that mostly hides her face. She's standing right beside Lisa, and as Yumi watches, she puts a finger to her lips.

Abruptly, pain explodes in Yumi's right leg, and the world rushes back in. She parried Allory's latest chop, yes, but the furious woman has shoved through the defense and smashed her saber into Yumi's thigh. She staggers, sword falling wide, as the judges start shouting "halt," but Allory has no intention of doing any such thing. She slashes at Yumi's unprotected facemask. Yumi recoils just enough to avoid being punched by Allory's saber guard, and instead the blade hits her right over the ear hard enough to daze her. Worse, the metal wraps around the mask and tags the back of Yumi's head, which bursts with shrieking pain. The sensor goes off, and the judges shout to stop Allory from following this up with another cut at Yumi's helpless head.

The audience hesitates in collective shock for a second, then erupts—some of it into cheers, some into protests, and Yumi even hears some boos, though all the sound is muted as though she's listening while underwater. Allory smirks down at her, flicks her saber out to the side in a dismissive gesture, and stalks back to her end of the piste. Dizzily, Yumi tries and fails to stand—she can barely hear anything over the buzzing.

One of the officials is saying something to her, kneeling, his hand on her shoulder, his face in her face. At first, it's startling, and her first impulse is to counter-attack, but she sees his expression is honestly concerned. "—all right?" he asks. "Ms. Kujikawa?"

Yumi nods, making the whole facemask shake. It's suddenly stifling, and she flails, trying to take it off. The official helps, and she can breathe again, chest heaving. Her leg is pumping with pain, which keeps resonating through her head.

"Are you hurt?" he asks. "Let me see your head?"

Her head. Yumi reaches back with her ungloved left hand and feels slight damp under her mass of silver hair. Allory's saber broke the skin.

"I'm ok," she says, teeth gritted.

"Are you sure?" His eyes are full of worry. "You can continue?"

"Yes." She looks at him directly, her red eyes burning into his. "Yes."

At length, he nods, rises, and turns back to the judges. She doesn't hear what he says, because she looks back to the stands. Lisa looks worried, her fingers turning white as she clenches the rail, but Danielle has vanished. That's something at least.

Still, it happened. What was Danielle trying to say? Does she want Yumi to throw the match, like Allory does, or what?

Whatever. Like *hell* is Yumi going to let Allory win after that.

Fire lights inside Yumi's core. Muramasa calls to her, reminding her of its hunger and the power it offers. She works to push it out of her thoughts, mostly managing it. Her leg hurts like hell, and she walks in a small circle, trying to shake it out.

Allory is arguing with the officials, who aren't giving her a point for the touch. The second she hit Yumi in a non-scoring area—on the thigh—the pass was dead, so no matter how many times Allory hit her afterward, she couldn't score a touch. So the shot to her facemask was utterly unnecessary and is grounds for a penalty. Finally, the rules win out, and Allory's lucky she isn't disqualified for bad sportsmanship. She stomps back to her corner, pissed. Her

Everyman Hat fans are on their feet, booing and hollering, and no amount of explanation from the fencers in the stands about the rules is going to quiet their anger—not when their "Aryan princess" isn't getting rewarded for injuring the uppity Asian girl. At least Nationals has security, and they start escorting red-faced bigots out of the venue.

Yumi's got to focus on taking out her own bigot, and she's at the other end of the piste.

From day one at Cobalt City University, a year and a half ago, Yumi knew she and Allory Greene were never going to get along, let alone be friends. She knew the type: the perky blonde cheerleader with the silver cross on her necklace and the wry comment to make behind your back. Not to disparage blondes or cheerleaders or even religious types—Yumi has known excellent examples of all three—but planting all three of those flags in one mean girl turns what might have been white flags very red. Sure enough, Allory Greene didn't disappoint—and the casual homophobia doesn't hurt, either.

Screw the threat. Screw the country. Screw the tournament.

Yumi's going to teach her a lesson.

They take up their on-guard positions, and Yumi sets her teeth against the pain in her leg. The bent down stance isn't the easiest, particularly when one of your legs is partially numb. She's got to stand up straighter than proper form would dictate, and she can see Allory taking note of it across the piste—sensing weakness. Bitch probably thinks she has a chance.

"Fence!" the judge says, and Yumi comes out advancing.

She doesn't use her powers—she doesn't need to. Allory is so surprised at Yumi's aggressive approach that her defense falters and she doesn't make an easy stop-thrust. Instead, she defends herself, parrying Yumi's threshing attack, but not riposting fast enough when Yumi comes back around with another slash. She's on the defensive, continuing to give ground until she steps off the piste, and the judges call a halt.

"If you're trying to lose," Allory says as she walks away, "you're doing a really shitty job."

Yumi doesn't say anything, but just heads back to her end of the piste. She almost turns her back on Allory, which would be a penalty to her, but she doesn't want to award this bitch any more touches.

Allory scores another touch, using her superior reach to get around Yumi's saber and hit her in the wrist again, right where she hit before. It's all her epee training—she's used to going for the tiny touches, not the clear, major hits—but it works halfway in saber.

They take up their places for what Yumi intends to be the final pass.

"On guard?" the judge asks. They both nod. "Fence!"

This pass moves slower, and Yumi doesn't consciously try to stop her power. She sees Allory coming on, cautious but forceful, and knows exactly what to do. Allory is going to try and draw the parry again, counting on her quick, detailed wrist work to get the touch. Or she'll do the coupe again and go over Yumi's guard. Neither is gonna cut it. Not this time.

Yumi shifts to a high guard, ready for a prime parry. That kind of defense can be intimidating for a less accomplished fencer, but Allory doesn't look concerned. She comes forward, ready, and slashes—a quick, precise blur of steel that Yumi could parry ... but she doesn't.

Instead, she drops low, narrowly ducking the slash, her knees nearly touching the piste, and explodes forward on her good leg, catching herself on her injured one, and thrusts her saber forward like a foil.

It's an insane move, one that leaves her back wide open, but it catches Allory off guard. The saber stabs into her with a satisfying impact, and she starts to fall backward, the way her body was already moving. Yumi watches her fall in slow motion, and stands up abruptly, sword slashing through the wire that holds Allory's saber to her jersey, then flicks back to knock the saber free of Allory's hand. It flips around and she catches it in her left hand, leaving her standing over Allory, a saber in either hand, as her team captain falls flat on her butt on the piste.

The sensor goes off, the judges wave, and Yumi takes the fifteenth touch.

"You stupid bitch," Allory says, glaring up at her in disbelief. "You don't even know what you've done."

"Kicked your ass?" Yumi says. "Yeah."

She carelessly tosses Allory's saber down next to her, turns, and walks off.

~

Her phone is already lit up with notifications when she gets to the locker room. Tweets and emails expressing bewilderment and asking for a comment. They aren't Allory's bombshell tweet itself—she isn't tagged—but rather responses to it. She has at least fifty notifications, most of them about this tweet.

Yumi takes a breath and looks at the source. It takes a second to load—connectivity isn't great here, but she can see it has two thousand likes and a quarter as many retweets already.

The tweet isn't what Yumi expects. Yeah, she expected the poorly lit footage of her outfitted as Muramasa, burning red katana drawn, fighting that asshole in the park just before she came to Nationals. She saw that on Allory's phone yesterday. The tweet has the same hashtags as yesterday but has one word added: "coincidence?" It's the same video, but this time it's intercut with an old fashioned and slightly grainy recording of another fencer, this one fighting foil against an appropriately attired opponent. The movements look similar enough to the untrained eye, and the fencer is incredibly fast. It looks vaguely familiar, and finally she sees the distinctive "1998 USFA Nationals" sign behind the piste. When Yumi gets it, her eyes widen.

"No," she says. "No, no, no—"

Sure enough, one of the fencers wins the bout, and a split-second after the electric sensor dings, she turns her back on her opponent and starts hopping in an ecstatic circle. Yumi's heart sinks and breaks entirely when the fencer pulls off her mask to reveal the smiling face of a thirty-ish Japanese woman, her silver hair carefully tied back, with distinctive red eyes.

Kujikawa Eiko.

The whole thing is about twenty seconds, and Yumi watches it again. Halfway through the third time, the phone falls out of Yumi's hand and clatters to the floor. There, it keeps buzzing with new notifications.

The implication is clear: capes have infiltrated professional fencing, starting with Eiko. And Yumi is Eiko's daughter.

76

The silver hair to honor her mother, which seemed like such a great flourish of defiance, now only plays right into that. God *dammit*.

Yumi smashes the locker closed hard enough to hurt her hand, and only then does she see someone standing not too far away, blocked by the open locker.

It's the last person Yumi wanted to face.

"Is it true?" Lisa asks, cradling her tablet. She looks very official—the team manager, not her friend or her girlfriend. "About you having, um, powers?"

Yumi bites her lip. She nods.

"Ok." Lisa expels a sigh, whether of exasperation or relief, Yumi can't say. "Uh, thanks for telling me."

"Lisa, I—"

Yumi takes half a step and reaches out for her, but Lisa turns away and looks at her tablet.

"I, uh, checked with the review board for an announcement," Lisa says, assuming the careful, analytical tone she takes on when discussing politics or the law. "Assuming these allegations are true ... well, it wouldn't look good that you hid your powers from the review board, but I think it's understandable, under the circumstances."

"It is?" Yumi feels a little twinge of hope.

"With Lyle Prather in the White House and superheroes constantly becoming less legal? Uh, yeah." Lisa swipes through some pages on her tablet. "Whenever an allegation like this is made, they have to take it seriously, and now they're reviewing footage of the bouts—not just yours, everyone's. As I understand it, if they decide you *do* have powers, it comes down to two questions: one, is your power-set relevant to fencing, which it absolutely is, and two, did you *use* your powers in any of your bouts."

"I didn't. I didn't need to, but—" Yumi trails off. "It's complicated. Some of my power is under my control, some of it's just how my body works. I'm fast, and my balance is perfect."

"Are you sure that's powers, or is it training? You said you started gymnastics when you were four."

"Three," Yumi says.

"That's a *lot* of training." Lisa looks away, back to her tablet. "Legally, this could be dicey. The Department of Homeland Security isn't a big deal. The Department of Superhuman Affairs, though—" She shakes her head. "I'm not sure what would happen."

"They could arrest me, right? Put me in a camp or something?"

"I doubt it," Lisa says. "You're a natural American citizen, and more importantly, your father is the head of a major corporation. I don't think Prather wants to go to war with K2 Aerospace. But—" She sucks in a breath. "This is going to look bad."

"What do you mean?"

"They're going to spin this," Lisa says. "Superhumans sneaking into a national sports competition. Unfair advantage over baseline humans. It's not going to be another BS line about trans people in bathrooms, of course, but same idea. Make people paranoid. Afraid. Make them distrust capes. It feeds Prather's narrative."

"Goddammit," Yumi says. "Maybe I should withdraw. Just forfeit the competition, like Allory wanted."

"It's too late," Lisa says. "The bomb's already gone off. If you forfeit, you're just proving them right, proving that you're the cape, and they get what they want anyway."

"I could quit in protest. Say I'm upset that someone's cheating—"

But she knows right away that won't cut it either. Maybe she won't take the heat, but she'll be a liar and a cheat, when she's trying so hard not to be. And she'll be flipping off all her fellow capes. Even so ...

"I just—I don't care anymore." Anger churns inside Yumi. "Fuck all this. I'll just leave. I'll—"

Lisa rounds on her in a much more direct way than she's ever faced her before. "This is your dream, isn't it? What about the Olympics? You talk about that all the time."

"The Olympics. *Shit.*" Yumi shakes her head. "I only took up fencing because of my mother, and—" Tears well up, and she can't stop them anymore. "Oh God, my mother. I'm doing this for her, and—and—"

"Hey." Lisa lays her hands on either side of Yumi's face, turning Yumi to look at her. "It's all right. Ok? It's going to be all right."

"It—it is?" Yumi looks up at her, blinking through the tears, and their eyes meet.

"You are a human being," Lisa says. "You have every right to do what you love."

Yumi doesn't know what to say. Instead, she leans forward a little and shuts her eyes, hoping that ...

Lisa's lips meet hers, and they kiss.

It's not one of the aggressive, passionate kisses they shared last night, but something soft and warm and sweet and exactly what Yumi needs. Tears stream down her cheeks, and she kisses Lisa again. Then they lean their foreheads together and just breathe for a second.

"Thank you," Yumi says. "I don't—I don't know what I'd—"

"Hey," Lisa says. "You're there for me, I'm there for you. That's how this works."

"So ... you're not mad?" Yumi asks.

"Mad?" Lisa looks at Yumi like she's lost her mind. "My girlfriend's a superhero. That's awesome."

"So I'm your girlfriend."

"Didn't we establish this?" Lisa asks.

"I think so?"

"Do you need a reminder?"

"Hell yeah."

~

That night, Yumi has lots of trouble getting to sleep. Lisa cuddles up to her back, a warm, reassuring presence that lets Yumi drift, hardly connected. But sleep itself seems elusive, and it's not just nerves. She can't shake the feeling that she's walked into something much bigger than her—much bigger than any of them.

Around midnight, she becomes aware of a dark figure standing in the doorway, one she can't see clearly. The Melting Woman seems to realize Yumi is watching her and steps through into the living room and out of sight.

Carefully, Yumi slips out of Lisa's arms and out of bed. She pulls on the hotel robe and treads gracefully toward the living room. As she does, she puts out her right hand, and Muramasa appears in her fingers. The steel has its usual crimson sheen but otherwise waits, quiescent and anticipatory.

The living room is full of guttering candles dripping all over the tables, chairs, and couches. The TV is covered in wax, which hangs down its screen like slime or lichen.

"Come out," Yumi says. "Face me."

She sees movement in the black screen and turns, only to find the Melting Woman looming right in front of her, and one disintegrating hand closes around her throat. The hand is cold and clammy, but there's little strength there to choke her. She can still breathe. Still speak.

"I'm not—" Yumi manages to say. "I'm not afraid of you anymore."

The rotting woman's face is just inches from her own, and the smell surrounds them. It fills the room, choking her, making her eyes water. It's the first time she's seen the Melting Woman face to face like this, this close, and it is every bit as horrifying as she could have imagined. The flesh runs off her face in rivulets, leaving slick red underneath, cheekbones going flaccid, teeth curling outward and falling out. The eyes are the only thing that remains—eyes that burn into her, demanding and accusing.

"I'm done with you," Yumi says. "Leave."

The Melting Woman's mouth moves, but no words come out. Nothing Yumi recognizes as words, anyway. The sounds just slur together into a lip-smacking muddle.

"Never," she finally says.

Then the arm weakens, she slumps toward Yumi, and her bulk crushes her against the wall. Slowly she dissolves, hissing and spitting and burbling, and Yumi turns her face away, trying not to be sick. The Melting Woman has no strength, but she has weight, and it holds Yumi in place for a long, long time.

Finally, she has melted enough that Yumi can snake out from under the bulbous mass. She stands there, watching and struggling to breathe in the stench, and stares at the dissolving blob.

"Never," the Melting Woman says again, her voice bubbling away.

CHAPTER 7

Some of the unpleasant heat bakes off Baltimore by night, but the muggy humidity extends well past dusk. Tonight it's at least ninety percent, making Yumi simmer as she perches atop the Transamerica building overlooking the convention center far below. The lights of the city live in a haze along the streets, as all that water in the air settles down into a sort of fog. It should be nice out, but it feels like melting. Inside the suit, it's worse—almost suffocating. She sits, cross-legged, the sheathed sword across her lap. Waiting.

"Couldn't sleep?" Danielle Swain steps out of the night behind her. "Maybe you're anxious."

Yumi stands slowly, deliberately, and turns to face Danielle, one hand on the hilt of Muramasa. She takes a casual defensive posture and glares out through the modified kendo mask.

Danielle has no such outfit—not even a tactical harness. Instead, she wears jeans, a fashionable white top, and sensible flats. She might have come straight from the bar. Pointedly, she has no sword, gun, or any visible weapon. She doesn't seem like she came looking for a fight, in stark contrast to Yumi in her full costume.

The assassin also doesn't look at all uncomfortable, and even smiles slightly. "That outfit looks hot."

"It is." Yumi refuses to rise to the bait. It's both hot *and* uncomfortable. "I see you dressed for the weather. Not even a mask."

Danielle shrugs, letting her sleeves billow a little. "I'm not ashamed of who I am."

Maybe you should be, Yumi thinks but doesn't say. She grits her teeth at the implication.

"Speaking of which," Danielle says. "Is it really wise, wearing that outfit here? At Nationals?"

"Everyone thinks I'm here already," she says.

"Ah yes. Thanks to your captain's tweets. Allory Greene, right?"

"Did she hire you to draw me out?" Yumi asks. Out of where, exactly, she leaves unsaid.

"Like she could afford me." Danielle stretches like a cat. "*Greene*. Isn't that a Jewish name?"

"What's your point?" Yumi shrugs. "I didn't think the Factory was fascist too."

"Funny," says Danielle, brushing one of her locs out of her face. "We're beyond politics."

"Sure you are."

"Speaking of politics, all those white supremacists in the crowd today sure are idiots, aren't they?"

"Now you're just being redundant."

"I could kill this Greene person, you know. Call it a professional courtesy."

"Thanks—" Yumi catches herself before she says she's tempted. "Hard pass."

Danielle shrugs. "So what's the occasion? For the costume?" she asks, like she doesn't know.

Yumi takes a deep breath and centers herself. She has to be utterly clear and unambiguous about this.

"What happened today," she says. "That will not happen again."

Danielle smiles, a joke about "winning" or "spanking some white girl" on her lips, but she draws up short. "You mean your nerdy little girlfriend."

"She's a *geek*, not a nerd. And yes. You touch her, and that's it. I'm done. The next time I see you, I kill you. Are we clear?"

Danielle's body language stays solid, unassuming, but something flashes across her eyes. "You think you can beat me."

"Maybe not," Yumi says as Danielle slowly approaches her. "Maybe you win, or maybe it's a draw. But odds are, one or both of us is too injured to be of any use to the Factory." They're face to face now, and Yumi has to look up slightly to meet Danielle's eye. "You'll fail your mission."

"So you're still thinking about it."

82

Dammit. Why does Danielle always have to twist things like this? She is entirely too clever. And skilled. And sexy. *Damn.*

"It's about to rain," Danielle says. "I can feel the pressure changing."

"What?" Yumi smirks. "No, you can't."

Rather than say anything else, Danielle reaches forward, despite Yumi poised to cut her down. It has the same tension as reaching down into a garbage disposal, while someone else's hand hovers over the switch.

It would be so easy: just draw the sword, slash across, and sheathe it all in one fluid motion. Less than a second. It would be a perfect iaijutsu strike. Muramasa hungers for it.

And yet, Yumi doesn't strike—it's all she can do not to tremble.

And when Danielle pushes Yumi's mask up onto her forehead, the evening breeze feels wonderful on her sweaty face, right before warm drops fall on her nose and her cheeks. In heartbeats, a light rain starts to come down, spattering Danielle's perfect white outfit and wicking off Yumi's costume.

"Dani—" Yumi starts.

"Don't call me that." Danielle continues to lean forward, and Yumi's lips part.

"Why are you here?" Yumi asks.

That makes Danielle pause. "Isn't it obvious?" Danielle runs her callused fingers along Yumi's cheek, wiping away the raindrops. Her caresses burn like knives.

Yumi pulls away—just enough to be out of easy reach, but not all the way removed. There, she stands her ground. Muramasa's fire burns within her, but it isn't warning her of impending danger. What does the sword want?

"Be real with me. You told me you felt free. That the Factory lets you be who you are and do what you want. So—" Yumi shrugs. "Why are you here? Is it to win Nationals, or is it to recruit me?"

Danielle smiles a wicked little smile. "Can't it be both?"

"No."

At first, Danielle sucks in air to laugh, but then she takes one look at Yumi's flat expression, and the mirth dies away. "You're serious."

Yumi nods. "You're either here because you want to be, or because the Factory sent you. Are you really free?"

"Hmm." Danielle turns her head slightly, thinking.

More rain comes down, making Yumi's mussed up hair wilt slightly, running off her chin and falling to the rooftop. As they fall, the drops slow, and Yumi can feel that same pressure in her head as when she watched Danielle activate her powers. Their powers call to each other and entwine.

If it's ever going to happen, it's going to happen now.

Come on. Yumi's heart beats faster, almost loud enough to hear. She feels a beat in her ears. *Come on.*

Danielle's lips part.

Which is when the black helicopter appears over the edge of the building, rising from where it must have hovered just out of sight. The chopper's big, more like a troop carrier than a gunship. Yumi can hardly believe she didn't hear it, but the pressure variation in her ears must have been due to the rotor blades. She manifests her will, and Muramasa appears in her hand, held just out to the side, leaving a trail of fiery red energy in a bending semi-circle from her scabbard to her hand. Because she summoned it rather than drew it, it doesn't pass through Danielle and cut her in half, and Yumi can feel the sword's frustration at that fact. She shoves her mask back into place and falls into a defensive stance.

"This isn't me." Danielle's eyes widen slightly, startled.

If it's an act, this interest in Yumi—or, y'know, her apparent surprise at the arrival of the helicopter—it's a good one. Yumi's met clinical psychopaths before in her line of work, and most aren't that polished.

The chopper rises over the rooftop, still almost entirely silent, and half a dozen black cords unspool, followed shortly thereafter by men and women in black spandex assault gear, two descending each rope. Their faces are covered, and they wear night-vision goggles that glow with thin streaks of red light. They bristle with weapons ranging from tactical katana to shuriken, from the man who unspools the chain of a kusari-gama to the woman who unfolds and extends a compacted naginata. In short order, Yumi and Danielle are facing a dozen ninja arrayed against them. No one speaks a word, but as Yumi points her sword at first one, then another, each ninja makes a hissing sound like an angered viper.

She's about to make a move when Danielle interposes herself, arms wide, her back to Yumi. The gesture is both protective and a little threatening—toward the ninja, not Yumi.

The rain grows heavier, plastering Danielle's clothes to her muscular frame and dripping down her locs. Yumi can hear the rain hammering down on her mask, but very little moisture gets in. The helicopter blades stir up a tiny hurricane, sending water flying in all directions.

The last to descend from the chopper is a well-built black man in an immaculate white suit, complete with a scarf and fedora that the rain doesn't seem to touch. As he walks, he clicks an ivory cane against the rooftop in an uneven rhythm. He looks like something out a period piece movie about the Jazz Age, and Yumi is so struck by his appearance that he's already on the rooftop, rolling forward with a predator's gait, before she snaps out of it. She's seen him once before, very memorably—he did try to kill her, after almost killing Sensei Sakuto.

Nathaniel Killdeer. Near as she can tell, he's the leader of the Factory.

"That will do, Agent Nemesis," he says to Danielle. "Your mission is over. Step aside."

Agent Nemesis? Yumi's glad the mask hides her goggling expression.

"Director, I have this," Danielle says.

"Maybe. But you are moving too slowly, and the Council wants results." He signals his ninja, half of whom draw their swords as one, while those in the back rank lift their rifles. "You are relieved of this mission. Please."

He has impeccable posture and enunciation, entirely without contractions, but with a tiny hint of a warm accent. Caribbean, maybe? South African? Yumi can't tell, and her heart is thudding hard enough that she doesn't have time to consider. He wears no obvious weapon, other than the cane that is clearly more an affectation than a mobility aid. If even half of Sakuto's stories are true, he doesn't need one. Standing unarmed at the head of a dozen ninja, he is clearly the most dangerous person here.

Rather than step back, though, Danielle raises her hands in a combat kata. She leans back into an unarmed defensive posture. What is she doing?

The ninja point their assault rifles at her with practiced, synchronized precision. Killdeer raises a hand to stop them.

Muramasa is hot in Yumi's hands, and her heart beats faster and faster. She tries to focus, like Sakuto taught her. See things clearly. Fight smart. Control the fear. *Control.* She stands behind Danielle, trying to steady her breathing. She needs the rest of the team, but even if she could get to her phone, not even Johnny Turbo could get from Cobalt City to Baltimore before it's all over anyway.

"Miss Swain." Killdeer frowns slightly and casually pushes open his suit jacket, revealing the pearl-white handle of a sword at his belt. "There is no purpose in you suffering injury, and I would hate to lose you as an asset. We will take Miss Kujikawa into custody regardless of your efforts."

"Maybe." Danielle looks around at the ninja arrayed against them. She speaks without emotion, with the cold assurance of a hardened killer. "How many of your assets do you want to lose tonight?"

The reasonable expression disappears from Killdeer's face, and the next words are sharp steel. He's gripping his sword now. "Stand down, Agent Nemesis. That is an order."

The world drags as their powers activate together once more, and the raindrops slow down around them.

Yumi thinks for a second that Danielle might charge him, but instead she relaxes up out of her stance, then draws up to attention with obvious reluctance. She stands at a kind of parade rest, hands crossed behind her back, and bows stiffly at the waist—a gesture Killdeer acknowledges with a slight nod. Apparently, she's changed her mind. Yumi starts to speak, but Danielle gives her a glance over her shoulder: a regarding look, flat and devoid of sentiment. The world rushes back in with such suddenness it makes Yumi catch her breath.

Now she really *is* alone.

"Yes." Killdeer says. The word contains no relief, only acknowledgment. "Lay down the sword, Miss Kujikawa. Do not worry, it will remain your sword—assuming we come to an arrangement. No one else of this generation can wield it, after all."

"You're—" Yumi's voice cracks. She bends down, compressing through the knees, and lays the burning Muramasa on the rooftop.

86

The flames gutter and mostly subside. "You're not just going to kill me and take it, huh?"

"Of course not," Killdeer says. "Had that been the plan, we would have shot you both from over there." With the same hand he used to stop the shooting gallery, he gestures first to a distant building, then toward Yumi, and the six ninja with hand-to-hand weapons drawn stalk forward.

Yumi's gaze flicks to each of them in turn, then to Danielle, where she's walking toward Killdeer's side with her hands folded at the small of her back. One hand is closed in a tight fist. Is that a sign or some kind, or just some weird Factory protocol?

"You're not going to try to talk me into it, huh?" Yumi asks. "Joining the Factory, I mean?"

"We have moved beyond that," Killdeer says. "Now the only question is how difficult the onboarding process will be for you."

Yumi's watching him—only a fool looks away from their enemy, Sakuto taught her—but when Danielle reaches his side, her fist abruptly opens. Yumi can feel their powers calling to each other again.

This is the moment.

"Hard pass!" Yumi summons her will, and Muramasa appears in her hand, painting whirling lines of fire through the air.

The ninja spring to the attack, reacting as if they expected it, but with her powers, their speed advantage goes away. The numbers, though, are still on their side, and Yumi skips back to one side to cut their paths to her.

At the same instant, Danielle lunges for Killdeer, and he pulls back in defense, not surprised. In their slow-motion world, he moves at normal speed. He smashes his open palm into her chest so hard and so fast ripples pass through her and through the rain, and the force sends her tumbling back to land shakily on her feet.

"Dani!" Yumi calls, but Danielle puts out her hand to wave her off.

She shrugs back her locs around her soaked shoulders, and Yumi sees she has a thin, straight sword with a handle that looks like that of Killdeer's cane in one hand. The director seems to realize it at the same instant, holds up the foreshortened cane from which she drew the weapon, and makes an annoyed face.

"Well?" he says, waving. "Take them."

Then it's entirely on.

With a sudden cry, Yumi charges into the oncoming ninja when they're a few steps away, hoping to break up their momentum, but they're well-trained, and she only catches one off guard. She smashes her sword into the ninja's guard hard enough to knock him off-balance to the side and drops low to sweep his leg. At the same time, she turns her head so a sword swipe narrowly misses her hair, rather than decapitating her. She throws herself into a forward somersault as the kusari-gama snaps through the space where she just was, its chain snapping raindrops out of the air. She keeps moving, coming up just in time to dodge a slash from the naginata, sucking in her stomach to avoid being disemboweled. She falls on her backside, free hand on the roof to keep her balance.

The world slows, and she yanks her hand away as bullets explode into the roof right there. Dodging, she hears the short burst of suppressed automatic fire, but Killdeer cuts them off with a shout.

"No guns," he says. "We take her *alive*."

Good to know.

The naginata comes for her again, and she catches it on Muramasa, locking the hooked blade out wide, but only then does she realize she played right into a trap. The ninja twists her naginata expertly, tearing Muramasa from Yumi's grasp and sending it spinning across the rooftop. Yumi starts in that direction, but she has to pull up short as a kunai cuts through the night, scraping off her armored forearm. The naginata's butt slams into her belly then whirls around for a killing blow, and she catches the haft in both hands to keep the blade end from gouging out her face. Even so, the ninja shoves down on her, clearly a woman of superior strength, and the blade inches closer. Meanwhile, the other ninja approach her, whirling their weapons, ready to stab their immobilized foe.

What happened to *alive*?

Then something strikes in their midst, scattering the ninja like frightened birds. A bloody sword point bursts through the naginata wielder's chest, and her body stiffens, then slumps aside. Danielle Swain stands there, blood spattered all over her hands and white shirt, Killdeer's slaked sword slipping out of the ninja. She stares down at Yumi, her wolf's eyes furious, and extends her free hand.

Yumi takes it, shivering slightly at the touch, like electricity between them.

As Danielle pulls her to her feet, she summons Muramasa, which appears in her hand, fiery red arcing in a path from where it fell. She holds the flaming sword low as Danielle takes a high stance against her back. She feels strong and reassuring.

The ten remaining ninja close around them, hissing.

No words pass between them, but Yumi and Danielle know exactly how to move. As one, they reverse their stances, meeting the incoming ninja with speed and accuracy. Even as their movements complement one another, their styles are utterly different. Yumi fights with fire and wind, quick and strong and passionate, while Danielle's style is grounded and fluid, like earth and water. Yumi does not stop moving, taking two steps with every strike and parry, while Danielle cannot be moved, relying upon her great strength to parry and throw back anyone who strikes at her. They fight together as though in a choreographed dance neither has ever learned but both know thoroughly.

Danielle drives a ninja with twin ninjato back with a mighty chop that shatters one sword and chips the other, while Yumi rolls over Danielle's back to cut first one, then another hurled kunai from the air, sending the blades spinning off into the night. A ninja with a katana rushes at them, blade high, and Yumi leaps aside just as Danielle barrels through, striking his hands from below even as the chop descends. His blade and his hands go floating through the night.

Yumi's style is marked by her ultimate restraint: she strikes her enemies with the pommel of her sword or its dull edge, or else takes them down with foot, hand, or elbow. She isn't here to kill anyone, even professional assassins. By contrast, Danielle holds no such compunctions: she spills blood, limbs, and bodies onto the roof. It should disconcert Yumi, watching the assassin so efficiently slaughter her own colleagues, but just at the moment, she doesn't have the space to think of anything but the fight.

Her mind is emptiness, her sword an extension of her body, her dance a reflection of herself. Danielle is the same. Her fury is rolling thunder. They move between the raindrops.

And together, they cut down one ninja after another, passing the attackers back and forth, an unstoppable and unfathomable flurry in the humid night. The world moves slower around them, and these ninja, though they outnumber them dramatically, are at a sore disadvantage.

The kusari-gama wraps around Muramasa and pulls, dragging Yumi toward that ninja. She holds tight to Muramasa, unwilling to cede her weapon, and fights to resist, but the ninja wraps the chain around her arms, pulling her inexorably forward. The dagger at the end of the chain thrusts toward Yumi's face, but she turns at the last second, abruptly reversing her momentum to snake around the ninja and pull her off-balance. She drags Muramasa along the ninja's leg, and the woman screams, blood flowing. Only when Yumi pulls free, finally disentangling herself, does she realize she has struck with the sharp edge of her sword.

And Muramasa is well-pleased. In fact, she can feel the sword demanding more—more blood, more pain, and even death—and it shatters Yumi's careful composure. She staggers back, blinking rapidly. "What—?"

Danielle hacks the deceptively slender sword across a ninja's chest, leaving a bloody trail in the air, and comes around facing her. "Move, Kujikawa," she says. "Move—"

Blood bursts and spatters Danielle's clothes as a bullet explodes into her thigh. She goes down instantly, as the limb goes numb under her, into a puddle of grime and blood. Yumi flinches, in surprise and in sudden pain, as though she's the one who got shot. She leaps in front of Danielle and whirls, blade raised, rage flowing from her.

Killdeer stands removed from them, a 9mm automatic smoking in his hand. He looks like he was about to shoot again, but now that Yumi's in the way, he holds his fire. Apparently, he really *does* want her alive.

They face each other across the rooftop as the rain drives down, flowing around the whipping blades of the helicopter. Yumi pants as she holds Muramasa up and ready, the blade burning with angry energy. Killdeer stands unassuming, his tie and white suit jacket flapping slightly in the breeze that's come up off the river. She doesn't know what he's capable of—the only time she saw him strike someone tonight, it was Danielle, and he knocked her ten feet with an open-handed strike. Yumi isn't as strong or tough as Danielle, and neither of them is nearly as skilled as Nathaniel

Killdeer, and yet she stands, unmoving, ready to fight him if she needs to.

At length, he breaks the stillness. "Withdraw," he says, and his ninja immediately obey. They head back to the helicopter, helping the injured walk, and hauling the bodies away.

"Running away?" Yumi asks, her voice like hot, brittle iron. "Scared to face me?"

Killdeer tilts his head slightly to the side, smiles superciliously, and turns his back.

For a second, Yumi considers pouring forth her power from Muramasa to strike him down. She's done it before: summoned forth fire, when her blade is sufficiently charged and furious. It wouldn't be wise, but just then, she doesn't care. What stops her, however, are memories of what happened the last time she struck without thinking—memories of the Melting Woman. That, and Danielle groaning behind her.

As soon as she's sure Killdeer won't shoot, Yumi hurries over to Danielle and kneels at her side. The woman is spitting and cursing and clearly in a lot of pain, which is reassuring. She isn't going into shock or anything. The rain has even let up, as the clouds part and Yumi can see the moon again.

"Where's Killdeer?" Danielle says. "The Factory?"

"They went all *get to the choppa*," Yumi says with a grin, feigning a really bad Austrian accent.

"What?" Danielle blinks at her.

"You know? 'Get to the—' You know what? Never mind."

Yumi reaches for Danielle, meaning to help her up, but the woman brushes her hands away and levers herself up of her own accord. She covers it well, but she's clearly favoring her left leg. Which is remarkable: she shouldn't even be able to stand, let alone walk.

"Are you ok?" Yumi asks. "You just got shot—"

Danielle gives her a dark look, and Yumi trails off. The assassin turns away and looks off over the bay, saying nothing. Rain starts to fall again, but not as hard—just enough to make her skin sparkle. Dammit.

"Thank you," Yumi says at length.

"I didn't do it for you."

"Ok." Yumi approaches slowly. "So why did you do it?"

"The Director was being an idiot," she says. "I didn't need his help. I don't need yours, either."

"His help doing what?"

Danielle turns to Yumi, and they're abruptly very close again. It feels very different from before, though: instead of longing and intimacy, Yumi feels only Danielle's mounting anger and pain. She was holding back, Yumi realizes, and it almost seems for a second that she's going to attack. Then Danielle drops Killdeer's bloody sword onto the roof.

"You better get to bed," Danielle says. "I want you at your best tomorrow."

"You can't be serious," Yumi says. "We're still going to fight?"

"Why not?"

"You just—" Yumi gestures at Danielle's mangled leg, which has swollen up but is, at least, no longer bleeding. "I mean, he must have missed your artery, but still. You need to go to the hospital."

Danielle sighs. "I'll be fine."

She starts to go, but Yumi reaches out and catches her by the sleeve, just over her elbow. Their powers activate again, and everything seems to go still around them. The raindrops float like tiny sparkling lights, reflecting the flame of Muramasa in Yumi's other hand.

"Thank you," Yumi says again. "Even if this is just an elaborate scheme to recruit me, you still fought hard for me. You took a bullet for me. Thank you."

Danielle opens her mouth, ready to dismiss that with snark, but instead she just says, "You're welcome."

Then she walks away into the dark and the rain, leaving Yumi alone.

CHAPTER 8

In the wake of Allory's "bombshell scoop," the tenor of Nationals changes overnight.

Walking out onto the arena floor, Yumi thinks the crowd has swelled to at least three times the size it was for the semi-finals, crammed with all kinds of unfamiliar faces and flashing camera phones. There's more press, too, and Yumi recognizes reporters from CNN, Faux, and all sorts of news organizations, many of them extremely right-wing. She sees representatives of Prather's old network—apparently the White House is formulating a "response" this morning, so that's great.

Whereas before, everyone had been generally supportive and enthusiastic, now they're loud and aggressive. Reporters both professional and amateur are leaning in to shout at her, demanding a comment on "the state of powered individuals in professional sports" or a response to the "allegations raised," or asking questions like "do you believe Muramasa is here at Nationals?" or the big one: "do *you* have powers?"

At her side, Lisa squeezes her hand. "It's ok," she whispers. "Allory didn't have the guts to name you. Doesn't want to be sued. So none of these people *know* anything—it's just rumors and speculation."

"Great." Yumi flinches away from camera phone flashes going off in her face and uses her warm-up jacket to shield them both from reporters. "That's so reassuring."

"Yeah." Lisa doesn't like all the attention either, but she insists on walking Yumi to the locker room. She's trembling, and not just from sleep deprivation. Yumi squeezes her hand back to reassure her. It seems to help, at least a little.

When Yumi came back from her encounter on the roof last night, she found Lisa asleep at the table in their suite, drooling a little on her keyboard, her computer displaying its lock screen. Apparently, she'd stayed up late to do more research, but it paid off. Apparently, while U.S. Fencing was all over anti-doping after the scandal a few years ago, their policies about powered individuals were very loose. It had just never come up in a serious way, other than Laser-Eye Louis winning bronze at the 2012 Olympics. But Louis's powers weren't relevant to fencing—burning your opponent with heat-vision during a bout isn't a winning strategy—and he never made any attempt to hide them.

This time, it's different. The news this morning said it had gone all the way to the IOC, who were "looking into the question." U.S. Fencing said they had received so many complaints and "concerned letters" that they were taking a hard look at all the National championship winners over the last two decades, including Yumi's mother, Kujikawa Eiko. Allory hadn't offered any proof of the allegations, and Yumi's mother had retired from public life a long time ago, even before her accident. To drag her into this—maybe take back her medals—it just made Yumi sick.

"I didn't mean for any of this to happen," Yumi says.

"I know," Lisa says.

She's tired, too. She didn't sleep well last night, even after she woke Lisa up at the table and hauled her back to bed. They just talked for a while until Lisa drifted off to sleep, cuddled up against Yumi's back. She lay there, mind churning, for what felt like hours, and only realized that she'd slept a little bit in retrospect, when the alarm went off and she woke up fully.

The media is utterly relentless, pushing against the staff in security shirts, who appear to have doubled since yesterday. Say this much for the NCAA and U.S. Fencing, at least they recognized the problem quickly and scrambled to address it. That helps her feel a little better, despite the waves of people in red Prather hats screaming at her. She is, after all, both Asian and a woman, which puts her fairly high on their hate-list. Even so, their anger isn't entirely directed at *her*, of course, but at the whole "corrupt liberal agenda" that's "scamming real Americans" by "sneaking illegals into sports."

WE ARE THE CHAMPIONS

As though Yumi isn't an American, or, more importantly, as though a *person* can be illegal.

The one fencer who might not be an American and *definitely* does some illegal things, however, doesn't seem the least bit concerned. Yumi sees Danielle Swain across the way when she gets into the arena where their final bout is to be held, and she looks refreshed and strong. She bounces back and forth between her feet, shifting her weight with a leonine grace that makes Yumi tingle with sympathetic recognition. Yumi doubts *she* stayed up for the last couple of days worrying about whether using her powers was cheating.

"It'll be ok," Lisa says. "Just focus on the match. It's fine."

Who's she trying to convince? Yumi, or herself?

Why not both?

If the Prat-hats are going to hate anyone, it's definitely Danielle. For one thing, she's Black, and not Black in a way that Prather and his fashy fanboys can safely ignore. No, today she came to make a statement: beads and jangling jewelry laced into her locs, her make-up fierce, and her colorful dress attention-grabbing. It's a *dress*, too—not her fencing gear—a reminder of just how femme she can be and is. Yumi realizes she's never seen Danielle in bright colors, and they suit her entirely too well.

Not that it should come as a surprise, but she also shows no sign of having been shot last night. She isn't even favoring one leg over the other.

Also, it's clear from the moment Yumi sees Danielle that she did *not* come to play. She has gone full heel: grinning and laughing and flipping off the Prat-boys, while their boos and jeers don't bother her in the slightest. She's not going to let these white supremacists forget that all their great white hopes were dashed in previous matches, including their anointed Aryan princess, Allory Greene.

No, this fight is between two queer women of color, the *best* at what they do, and *fuck* the haters.

"Oof," Lisa says in a whisper.

"What?"

"Maybe you should have dressed up, too," she says. "Like in a slinky black dress. Or a kimono."

Yumi nudges her. "You just want to see me in a kimono."

"Duh."

Lisa lets go of her hand, and Yumi heads up onto the dais to meet with the judges and her opponent. Danielle's energy is magnetic, and Yumi suddenly wishes she had that kind of confidence.

The ceremony before the finals is carefully choreographed and ritualized, a bit like the build-up to an MMA fight, but way more respectful. The two fencers meet and shake hands, while the announcer talks about them. It all feels surreal and distant, and Yumi basically doesn't hear anything he says. It all sounds like droning whale song. She can't quite believe she's here. Lisa, as her manager, says a few words—how does she seem so in control and calm?

Only when Yumi shakes hands with Danielle, feeling the firm grip of her callused hand, does Yumi lock eyes with her rival and see the dark humor there. She realizes that all of this—the ceremony, the flashy clothes, even the tournament itself—it's all performative for Danielle. It's all an act. And when it comes down to it, Yumi is doing exactly the same thing. They're both wearing costumes, even if they look like normal clothes.

Yumi has the sudden, unreasoning desire to grab Lisa and kiss her in front of everyone—make a real show of it. She can see the tweetstorms now, the endless hot takes that will be, at best, about the "lesbian fencers!", and "a great day for representation!", and, likely, much worse. She wouldn't be doing it for the right reasons, though: she'd just be using Lisa to steal some of the attention from Danielle's performance, and that wouldn't be fair to her.

Raincheck.

The ceremony over, they head down the dais to the locker rooms. Yumi is swarmed by people, including a bunch of CCU students who came down to see her, having produced flags with slogans like "Yumi Kujikawa: Daughter of Heroes!", or "Yumi 4 President", or "Yumi, I want your babies!", that kind of thing. She even receives well-wishes from other fencers she met along the way: Janine Marks and Lindsay Moorcock both come by to offer her encouragement and support, and not just because they want to see her beat Danielle. There's real camaraderie there, and Yumi thinks they'll be friends in the future.

Danielle, on the other hand, just slips through the crowd, shedding her attention-grabbing pretense, and disappears into the locker rooms.

Allory and Samantha are waiting outside the locker room. They both give Yumi knife-shaped glares, but ultimately Allory nods to her, and they pass by without incident. She may be a raging bitch, but at least Allory isn't an utter scumbag. That sort of softness is totally going to tank her career on right-wing news.

"What?" Lisa asks, always attentive. She touches Yumi's hand. "What's wrong?"

Yumi squeezes her hand, and they duck into the locker rooms where at least the crowd isn't watching. She looks around, and they seem alone for the moment.

"Are you ok?" Lisa looks so cute when she's concerned, her lips pursed and her eyes soft.

"Yeah." Yumi leans back against the block of lockers with a sigh. "Just—I'm a little nervous."

"You? Nervous?" Lisa smiles, as if she's about to laugh, then catches herself. "I'm sorry, that's just ... I mean, you're a superhero."

"Yeah, well, no pressure, right?" Yumi opens her locker and looks at herself in the mirror—under all that silver hair, she looks tired.

Lisa hesitates, seemingly uncertain how to handle this. She watches Yumi adjusting her hair for a second, then pulls out her tablet. "I know what'll cheer you up. Rule 34."

"What?"

The image Lisa shows her is not at all what Yumi expected: an animated gif of at least three vaguely anime characters having sex. She blushes furiously and stares, wide-eyed. "Lisa, what the—?"

"There's hentai of you!" Lisa says, beaming. "Well, of Muramasa, anyway—isn't that hilarious?"

"Hilarious?" Yumi isn't sure what to think as Lisa scrolls through image after image of a vaguely Japanese anime woman in black leather doing her thing with a number of faceless dudes. "More like creepy and weird and ... ok, that one's pretty good. Oh." She furrows her brow. "How is that one even physically possible?"

"I know, right?" Lisa says, then blushes. "I may have stayed up late for more than just research. A lot of people think you're a white girl. Or that you're out of some anime. It's kinda hard to tell—"

"*Lisa.*"

"What? It's not you—not really." Now she looks shyly down at her feet, chagrined. "It's just ... I, uh—"

Yumi frowns. "What?"

"I ... may have had a crush on you," Lisa says. "Muramasa, I mean. Before I knew, uh, who you were."

Yumi blinks. She never would have expected that, not in a million years. "Really?"

"Well, yeah. I mean—" She shows Yumi another picture, this one of Muramasa, sans most of her costume but for her mask, kneeling, turned away, one hand on the ground, her burning sword draped over one shoulder, looking back with come-hither eyes. "There aren't a lot of Japanese capes out there, especially not superhot ones like her. *You.* Since that first video, last year, I've had these ... fantasies—" She bites her lip and trails off.

Yumi takes her hands, but Lisa still doesn't look up. "Why are you telling me all this?" Yumi asks. "And why now?"

"Because—" Lisa finally meets her gaze, and her eyes are wet but determined. She takes a deep breath, and it all explodes out of her in a rush. "Because you are better than I ever could have dreamed and I need you to know that!"

They stand there, alone in the locker room and also the universe, and Yumi think she can hear their hearts beating in time at the same fast rate. She can feel the pulse in Lisa's hands and see it in her throat. And she feels ... reassured. And warm.

"Ok then," Yumi says.

"Ok," Lisa says.

"I ... I kind of want to say the other thing."

"The other thing?" At first, Lisa looks confused, then her eyes widen. "Oh." She flushes bright red. "Um ... maybe later?"

"Definitely."

Lisa squeezes Yumi's hands one more time, then heads off, leaving her alone in the locker room. There, Yumi breathes in deep and releases it in a sigh. She leans back against the lockers and looks up at the cracked ceiling. This whole tournament has been a roller-coaster ride, and it's almost over. One way or another.

"You heard all that, huh?" she asks.

Danielle doesn't need to announce her presence with something as cliché as a locker closing or a zipper hissing. She's just there, in her black fencing outfit, mask held idly in her hand. Her expression isn't one Yumi can easily read, as is often the case with her. There are emotions there, but they're buried deep.

"It was a nice dress," Yumi says. "Surprised you aren't still wearing it. If you wanted to seduce me."

"That old plan?" Danielle smirks. "I've given up on that."

"Because it didn't work?"

"Because it did."

Dammit. She walked right into that one. And it's totally true.

"So now you've decided to let me beat you, so that I'll decide to join you, is that it?" Yumi hides her unease with a confident smile. "Or wait, maybe *you'll* win, and then I'll be unable to forget about you, and I'll just have to seek you out? Or—"

"Honestly, that all sounds exhausting." Danielle sits down beside her, leaning against the lockers opposite, one leg bent, knee up. She pulls it in close to her chest, stretching. "I'd rather just fence."

"Yeah?"

Her wolf's eyes glitter. "Yeah."

They sit there in silence for a bit, as the clock ticks down to their bout. Yumi was nervous before, but now, the anxiety has faded into pleasant companionship. After their fraught encounter up on the rooftop, she expected ... she isn't sure what she expected, really, but it involved a lot more violence. Time enough for that later.

"Your girlfriend's cute," Danielle says at length.

"Thank you?" Yumi's not sure what to say to that. "I'll tell her you think so. Also, you touch her, and I'll cut your fingers off one at a time. And feed them to you."

"Noted." Danielle smiles. "You've told her about us, I assume?"

"Us?" Yumi looks away, trying to sound and look casually bemused. "What about *us*—?"

She feels Danielle's breath on her face and turns back in time for their lips to brush against each other. Their faces are almost touching, and Danielle's cold yellow eyes seem to churn with an inner hunger. She has leaned across, supporting herself with one hand on the locker beside Yumi, and whispers into her slightly open mouth.

"Are you sure about that?"

In that moment, Yumi knows two things: one, there is an "*us*," and two, unless she does something about it, this woman is definitely going to kill her someday—or vice versa.

"Will you get off?" Yumi asks.

"I hope so." Danielle's eyes narrow slightly.

Shit.

A source of heat burns in the narrow space between their faces, and flames lick up around their chins. The Muramasa blade, burning in Yumi's hand, floats just shy of Danielle's throat. Her skin starts to redden from the heat. The assassin doesn't flinch from the pain, but instead stares at Yumi as though daring her to go further.

"Get," Yumi says, "off."

This time, as she slides back, Danielle has the good sense to look a little chastened. That hunger in her eyes is still there, but now it has a violent edge to it. She doesn't like being rejected, and she's getting a little impatient. Yumi keeps the blade at her throat until they're both standing between the row of lockers, and she holds Danielle at bay at the full extension of her arm and sword. Her heart is racing.

The silence drags as they fight without moving, Yumi's fire smashing against Danielle's cool reassurance.

Do it, Danielle seems to be asking, and for a terrible, dark moment, Yumi almost does. There's something deep inside her—a voice, an impulse—that's been growing louder and more insistent this whole time. She tried to drown it out with fighting, with Lisa, heck, with Danielle, but it's there, and it's not going anywhere.

Because it's her.

Either of them is about to speak when a loud knock echoes through the locker room. "Five minutes, ladies," the attendant calls through the door, without looking.

Danielle steps out of reach of the sword, and Yumi lets her arm slide down to a low defense. She has no more words, but her expression says enough.

100

Yumi opens her designated locker, meaning to put Muramasa back in, then thinks better of it. She puts the blade in her long sports bag instead.

~

They take their places for the final bout of the NCAA Nationals, at the center of the vast convention hall space, both of them geared up in tight white outfits, each with a single white glove over their dominant hands while the other remains bare. Danielle's ambidextrous, and she's fighting southpaw today. Is she favoring her leg after all? Who knows.

The announcer eventually gives up trying to get the Prat-boys in the audience to shut up, and he signals the judges to attach their sabers while two more staff members hook up the wires to their jackets. Once the system is set up, Yumi thrusts and slashes her weapon through the air a couple times: light and malleable, not as well balanced as Muramasa but less ... hungry.

She can feel it in her own gut as well: that call from her sword to feed on the blood of a worthy opponent. She's keenly aware of Muramasa in her gym bag over on the sideline, where Lisa watches in rapt attention. She brightened up her hair for the occasion, and it looks like a brilliant rainbow in a sea of white cloth and blue mats. The look of expectation and faith on her face lights a little warmth in Yumi's chest.

She can do this.

When the announcements are done, the official instructs them to salute, and they do so, sabers whipping smartly through the space between. If anyone was expecting a flourish or scene, it doesn't happen. No revelation of silver hair or fire magic or anything: just two highly competent women coming together to test their skills.

Even before the announcer asks for it, the world quiets around Yumi—it doesn't fall silent, but the voices fade to a dull rumble. For now, right here, there's just Danielle and her. Just the two of them, alone in a universe built specifically for them. She crouches a little, summoning her strength and power into the core of her being, and Danielle does the same. They look totally different, see the world totally differently, they fight totally differently, but standing there, on the piste, both swords on the right side from Yumi's perspective, they might as well be mirror reflections of one another.

"En garde," the official says, opting for the classic French commands for this, the saber final. The third word stretches out: "Allez—"

The world turns sluggish around them, the official's hands slowly falling, and Yumi and Danielle activate their powers at the same time. They meet and flow around one another, entwining and entangling, feeding upon one another with fantastic results. Yumi's never seen the world slow quite this much, as though everything around her has suddenly stopped.

"What," Yumi says, and her voice has a distant, echoing quality. "What is this?"

Too late. Danielle is coming at her, saber seeking, and Yumi swats it away with a sharp, small flick of her wrist. The assassin falls back, and abruptly the world rushes back in around them, and she hears the audience erupt with shouts and gasps. They didn't see what happened—how could they?—but somehow the buzzer goes off, indicating that Danielle scored a touch. Only now, belatedly, does Yumi feel the hot pressure on her right arm where Danielle's saber snaked around and slapped her.

The judges look bewildered, and why shouldn't they? That's probably the fastest they've ever seen two fencers move, but because both of them went at that speed, it wasn't obviously unnatural for either one. Yumi can't credit how she knows this, but she sees it in their confused expressions that turn to a kind of impressed acceptance. Maybe everyone's perception sped up, just a little. Her head hurts.

Danielle's sword snaps up to point at her face, and it pulls Yumi back into the bout. She's down one touch to zero, but at least now she has a sense of what she's up against. That won't happen again.

Of course, she's utterly wrong.

They come together again, a little more cautiously this time, sabers seeking and flashing in the overhead lights. The murmurs of the crowd fill the arena, despite the judges' best efforts to keep them quiet, but Yumi focuses through the distraction. She breathes slowly and raggedly, forcing herself to stay calm. She increases her speed gradually to match Danielle, matching her parry for riposte, dodging her strikes and—

Danielle seems to stab right through her parry and rakes the blade along Yumi's arm and hits her on the shoulder. The sensor goes off, and Yumi's down zero to two. They retreat to their separate territories of the piste, and Yumi struggles to get her breathing under control. What just happened?

Of course. Danielle varied time. It's a novice trick—get your opponent accustomed to a particular pace for your exchanges, get into a rhythm, then suddenly go faster or, in this case, slower, and odds are they'll mess up their timing. It takes some luck and kinesthetic control, but Danielle has that in spades. Usually it's not *literal*, but when you can actually control time around yourself ... Yumi has used the same trick on dozens of opponents, usually opting for a sudden explosive move rather than a slow one, but whatever works. *Dammit.*

The crowd is louder now. Yumi doesn't expect any of them understood what happened, or at least they don't have any definitive proof. Danielle is subtle, and that point could be explained away by skill and luck. She hasn't done anything to out either of them yet.

"—Ready?" the official is asking. "Are you ready?"

Yumi nods. "Yes." Her voice sounds gravelly and harsh.

"En garde."

Enough of this.

"Allez!"

This time, Yumi engages Danielle's blade aggressively. Another duelist might have gone defensive, and Yumi's counting on Danielle to expect that. Instead, she catches the assassin a bit by surprise, launching a big attack but snapping the saber right back into line to protect herself without leaving an opening. She moves fast and hard, seeming to stalk toward Danielle, saber held horizontal at her face as they move along the piste. The audience can't see the lightning-fast slash-parry exchanges, because they're too fast for anyone but Yumi and Danielle themselves.

When Danielle gets to the end of the piste, she drops into a stop-thrust, but Yumi expected that. She leaps, the sword cutting under her curling leg, and lands at the same instant she snaps her saber against Danielle's mask with a satisfying *thwack*.

One to two.

The next pass doesn't go nearly that quick. Yumi's power matches Danielle's, but she must be tiring, because they only go a *little* faster than the average high-level fencer. Strike meets parry, riposte meets parry, Yumi slips a thrust and slashes, but Danielle ducks under it, and then they leap back at the same time. For a second, it seems like maybe the judge will call a halt, but Danielle utters a sharp growl and lunges at Yumi, the world slowing around them both. Yumi barely gets her saber up in time to block Danielle's strike, but not good enough. The blade whips around and tags her wrist.

One to three.

The pass after that is a long back and forth, cautious advance and quick retreat, dancing steps in a choreographed ballet neither of them know but both of them execute flawlessly. It goes on and on until two seconds remain on the clock for the first round, and Danielle launches a counter into Yumi's thrust, testing her resolve and courage. Mistake. Yumi perseveres, unwavering, and they hit each other at the same time. Yumi wins right of way and the touch.

Two to three.

They retreat off the piste at the end of round one, and the crowd—which hasn't been particularly quiet even during the passes—claps loudly. Yumi, sweating profusely inside her mask, almost forgot they were there. There's Lisa, on her feet, rainbow hair bouncing in her enthusiasm, as well as the other students from Cobalt City waving CCU flags and their signs, and Yumi's heart feels a little lighter. She glances at Danielle, who is staring down at her saber and making micro-adjustments to her grip. Up until just now, Yumi never really understood the Factory: last night, she saw its power and its horror, but today, she can see the true cost. Danielle doesn't have a student body to cheer her on, or a Lisa to come home to. Does she even have parents, champions or not?

All she can do is keep fighting.

Three minutes of fencing down, and only five touches, making it a low-scoring bout so far. In a sense, this is exactly the outcome any tournament is looking for: the two finalists should be extremely evenly matched. If anyone came into this thinking Danielle would smash Yumi like she has all her other challengers, they are sorely disappointed. Yumi doesn't intend to lose, and if she does, she's going to make Danielle work for it.

And if anyone was expecting round two to go like round one, that's *another* cause for disappointment.

Danielle comes roaring off the piste in round two with a non-crossing flèche, saber scrabbling, that almost catches Yumi off-guard. If Janine hadn't done almost exactly the same thing, Yumi definitely would have been touched. She's ready for it, though, and steps forward, to the side and past her, dragging her saber across high to low. They both end up off the piste, Danielle up tall with her saber low and pointed down, Yumi in a graceful crouch with hers pointed high. Going off the piste would have ended the point anyway, but the sensor on Yumi's sword has gone off and she got the touch before they went out of bounds.

The judges spend a full minute angrily discussing the dangerous move and whether they will allow it. Meanwhile, Yumi and Danielle stare at one another, neither willing to blink.

Three to three.

A quick exchange. Thrust, parry, riposte, disengage—narrow touch.

Three to four.

Athleticism and footwork marks the next pass. Slash, parry, twist, riposte, beat-parry, arms pumping and legs exploding—torso cut. Touch, Kujikawa.

Four to four.

A complex blur of attacks and blocks. Thrust, parry, riposte, counter, parry, thrust, parry, riposte and disengage, thrust, parry, ducked slash—just catches the mask. Touch, Swain.

Four to five.

It proceeds like that, back and forth and forth and back. Sometimes Danielle goes up two or even three, but Yumi catches her right back up. Most of the time they trade touches, and the score remains even.

Their bodies move as though molded together and broken apart only by accident. As though they were born to fight, or perhaps one birthed the other in fighting. They are reflections of one another—one the true face, one the shadow—and Yumi can no longer say which is which.

When the buzzer sounds the end of round two, Yumi realizes they've been fighting for six whole minutes, and she looks up at the score: eleven to eleven.

The crowd is on its feet at this point, and if she thought the cheering was distracting before, it has reached a fevered pitch now. In the space of what seemed like no time at all, it went from a low-scoring, cautious match to a fast, furious, violent contest between two expert fencers. Now, they take a break, but clearly neither of them needs it.

Blood thunders between Yumi's ears, and energy crackles through her limbs. She stands in perfect balance, bouncing back and forth between the balls of her feet as if she were light as a feather. She should be exhausted, but she isn't.

She's *hungry*.

Danielle is ready to come right back at her, and Yumi thinks she hears a faint growl from inside her mask. Only the judges stepping onto the piste keeps the two from hurling themselves back into the duel.

Let her. Let her *come*.

Somewhere in the back of her mind, she knows Lisa is calling her name—her fans are cheering for her—but she doesn't care. The judges are asking if she's ready, but their voices are muted, as though her ears are clogged.

"En garde!"

The rest of the world fades out, and Yumi just sees the piste, Danielle's sword, and Danielle behind it. Then it's just the sword and Danielle. Then just Danielle. Her enemy.

With a flick of her wrist, Yumi spins the saber in a flourish and snaps it in-line with her enemy's mask.

"Come on," she says, her whole being thirsting. "*Come on.*"

Danielle doesn't disappoint.

Even before the starting cry of "allez!" has faded, they meet in the center of the piste, hurling themselves into attacks at the same exact moment. It's Janine's move, only both do it at once. Swords meet and sing off one another in the center of the piste, and then they're tumbling past each other, airborne, blades clashing and crackling. Danielle twists in the air and attacks backward even as she falls, while Yumi reverses her saber in her hand and uses it to parry Danielle's slash behind her back. They both hit the piste,

Danielle on her back, Yumi on her side. Danielle kips up to her feet while Yumi rolls into a crouch.

Somehow, there was no touch.

The judges are shouting, but Yumi can barely make out the words. They both get a warning, because such a ridiculous dangerous move is way out of bounds, but it doesn't matter. Yumi's breathing hard and she can feel herself grinning like a lunatic. Somehow, she knows Danielle feels the same.

It's a long wait between passes this time, while the judges confer. Really, they should stop the bout right there, but since neither of the fencers was more to blame than the other, they let the warning stand. No touches awarded. Meanwhile, Yumi and Danielle are both heaving, staring at each other from their sides of the piste.

This was why she came to Nationals. Why she started fencing in the first place.

This.

Finally, the judge asks if both fencers are ready, and both give the customary nod. Tentatively this time, the judge says "en garde," pausing while they tense, then "allez!", but he doesn't have to worry. Nothing insane happens—unless you consider fencing faster than the eye can follow to be insane.

They meet near the middle of the piste, slightly closer to Danielle's end, in a clash of sabers and swaying bodies. There's no hesitation, no testing each other's defenses—not this time. They know each other, perhaps better than any two fencers in the history of the sport, and each is intimately familiar with the other's style.

It isn't about strategy or tactics or out-thinking each other. It's less of a fight and more of a dance—not because they know the steps but because their bodies create them together, and their minds surrender to the rhythm. They fight utterly differently but in perfect harmony.

After thirty seconds of nonstop clashing, Yumi is just too slow with a dodge, and Danielle gets a touch.

Eleven to twelve.

Yumi is ephemeral, striking like a hunting raptor borne aloft on the wind. Her fury and precision break up Danielle's strength and test the very limits of her solidity.

Danielle's defense isn't perfect, and Yumi takes advantage of that to spin an impossible thrust with her saber that narrowly eludes a solid block. Her blade bends on her rival's chest, and it feels as though Danielle's body draws toward Yumi, yearning for her.

Twelve to twelve.

Danielle's body is like a river: unstoppable and unending, nurturing its banks but consuming all that is caught in its middle. Her fluidity tempers Yumi's passion—it strikes when she oversteps, punishes her recklessness.

A stop-thrust catches her in the gut, and Yumi fairly loses control of herself entirely. Her world shakes, and she gasps, not just because of the touch. She smiles furiously within her mask.

Twelve to thirteen.

It all fades away: doubt, anxiety, regret. All of it, gone. She can't remember the last time she felt so good.

They are united on the piste, sweating and heaving and thrashing gloriously, burning their hands and feet as they dance. This is why they came to this place: to etch art from a world that moves so slowly by comparison it might as well be standing still. They came to create new life.

Yumi is no longer certain if they are fighting or making love, there, right in front of an arena full of astonished onlookers and the world at large.

Danielle is just slightly off with a parry, and Yumi's sword slaps her wrist.

Thirteen to thirteen.

Danielle is a mountain, as eternal as the earth from which she takes life, taller and more powerful than the feats of mortal women and men. Yumi's strikes bounce off her sword, and when she lands a strike to Yumi's middle, it is strong enough to knock her back two steps onto her backside.

There is no question about that touch.

Thirteen to fourteen.

Yumi's heart is a furnace, her fighting like fire, her strikes consuming and ushering in a tempest of rain in the desert. Her rage consumes Danielle's strength, diverting and demolishing it.

She doesn't want it to end, Yumi knows, as she's hacking down at Danielle's defense. She no longer cares how artful or beautiful the match looks. She wins the next touch, because she must. She can't let it end.

She thinks she will burst into flames on the spot and rise once more from the ashes.

Her saber wraps Danielle's and slaps against her mask, a strike that would have given a fencer in long-ago Germany a cheek scar worthy of pride and repute.

Fourteen to fourteen.

As she stands there, waiting for the next pass to begin, Yumi sees the world slow to a crawl around her, all but for Danielle, standing at the other end of the piste, shoulders heaving. One point to go—one last pass—and then it will all be over. Her body shakes from weariness and euphoria, and she perches on the edge of ruin. She's gasping, she's panting, she's alive and dying all at once.

Only then does Yumi see the smoke leaking from the seam of her glove, and from the collar of her jacket, and from her mask. How is no one else seeing this? Are they all seeing it?

Only then does she hear the roaring in the back of her mind— feel the hunger in her gut.

Muramasa calls. It demands. It will not be ignored.

Nor does Yumi want to.

This. This is the moment.

The moment where she calls the sword to her, cuts through Danielle's blade, and puts an end to their contest. An end to their rivalry. An end to her false face, with its false expectations and pressures.

In this moment.

An end, and a beginning.

New life.

"Allez—" the judge is calling.

"Wait," Yumi says. "Wai—"

But her breath chokes off as spectral hands wrap themselves around her throat. She looks up, and there is the Melting Woman, hovering just above and before her, flesh squidgy and drooping off a gelatinous skeleton. A shudder passes through Yumi, and all her joy and exhilaration turns to terror and horror. Her saber falls helplessly to the side, off-line to Danielle and presenting no threat.

She stands up on her toes, back arched, clasping with her free hand at her neck.

"Never," the Melting Woman says. "Never—"

Dimly, she sees Danielle coming toward her, stalking forward cautiously, like a predator who suspects a ruse. And why not? Yumi has the reflexes to snap the sword back in-line and catch her unawares. This could be just some bizarre feint, and if it is ...

"Dan—Dani," Yumi manages to choke out. "Wai—"

But the Melting Woman can be denied no more easily than the sword. She leans down, and for the first time, Yumi looks directly into her swollen, slippery face—the bloated cheeks sliding apart, the eyes burning to cinders, the teeth crackling and falling apart like the discarded petals of a dying flower.

"Never," the Melting Woman says, the words burbling. "Never forget—"

She sees the horror. She sees the pain. And she sees something she had not seen before.

Sorrow.

"I'm ... sorry," Yumi says.

And just like that, the Melting Woman is gone, leaving Yumi to collapse to her knees before Danielle. She's still on the piste, her saber is still in her hand, and the pass is still technically going. The last few seconds of round three are ticking away—Yumi can see the clock, dimly, behind Danielle's head. The crowd has fallen absolutely silent—no one knows what's going on.

Surely now is the moment. Her saber is uselessly wide—there's no way she can get it back in-line in time from this range. Danielle has only to reach out and thrust her saber into her wide-open chest.

But she doesn't.

"What," Danielle says, the word little more than an angry hiss. "What ... are you ... doing?"

Yumi remembers Lisa, and somehow, she can make out the sound of her fast, anxious breathing. The sound of her racing heart.

"I'm sorry," she says again, but not to the Melting Woman. "Sorry to disappoint you."

Then she lowers her head and bows to Danielle.

And just like that, the arena erupts. Yumi can't parse all the voices, but some are furious, some triumphant, and many are just overwhelmed with excitement. People have conceded matches before, of course, but no one expected that to happen this time, and in such a way, after such a bout. The judges are trying to be heard over the loudspeaker, urging patience while they sort out what just happened.

Yumi looks up at Danielle, who stands over her, saber raised. Danielle was fighting her at full effort, trying to pull this out of her and absolutely succeeding. And now, thwarted by a ghost? Yumi fully expects Danielle to strike her down—not just swat her or stab her with the saber, but drive it through her mask, into her face, and down through her body. And just then, her every fiber spent, her lungs slowly drawing breath, she almost welcomes it.

Danielle rips off her mask and looks down at Yumi furiously. At first, there's murder in her eyes, but then it softens. She's so guarded—so closed off—but today, in their bout that became an epic duel, Yumi saw something in her that she'd never recognized before, or even expected might be in her. Her work isn't yet done.

Slowly, Danielle lowers the saber, acknowledges her adversary with a curt nod, and steps back.

Then, as though that act broke some unseen barrier, people come rushing the piste to sweep the combatants up in congratulations, condolences, and a barrage of interview questions. Yumi smiles wanly as the other students fawn all over her—even Samantha, though Allory isn't here. She only has eyes for Lisa, though, and when the rainbow-haired girl appears, beaming, Yumi is glad to take her proffered arm.

"I'm sorry," Yumi says as they make their way to the locker room. "I'm sorry I let you down."

"You didn't," Lisa says, wiping away her tears. "You were amazing. You were amazing!"

Yumi glances past her to Danielle, still on the piste, still standing there. She's lowered the saber now, but it's still there in her hand. Her eyes are fire.

That's not what Yumi was apologizing for.

CHAPTER 9

Danielle Swain sits in the empty locker room, letting the tension of the fight ebb out of her muscles. Strength and soreness drain away at the same rate, thanks to the Factory's sorcery. The rituals were painful, like being born and dying over and over, but she endured them, and now she can endure anything. She's been shot, stabbed, burned, crushed, and fallen more than ten stories. She's taken wounds that should have killed her twice over. She's died and come back more than once.

None of them hurt like what happened today.

To fight so hard—to come so far—only to fail, in the moment where it all counted?

It's the failure that devastates her.

And it's not even the thought of reporting to Nathaniel Killdeer. He'll take her back, of course—he always has, and probably always will. She's one of the Factory's best operatives.

And there's plenty she can do, except, apparently, break Yumi Kujikawa.

She shouldn't be surprised, considering her heritage. Yumi springs from a line of champions, and she hasn't disappointed them yet. There's a reason the cursed sword chose a street urchin out of so many others who tried—others who tried and died. It was her power and will that had made the Silver Echo the finest killer in the Factory.

Before she found freedom and became the hero Silver Sakura.

Before she had a daughter, and if Muramasa serves the daughter, she must have the same power.

She's no longer alone in the locker room, Danielle knows, and she recognizes the presence as clearly as any perfume or familiar laugh. When they first met, she didn't think much of her, but now she knows better.

"Hey," Yumi says.

"Hey." Danielle looks up at her—at the lithe warrior's build, the crimson eyes, the silver hair showing black at the roots. Honestly, with as much fire as burns in that woman, it's amazing her hair isn't red.

She wonders where Yumi thinks her powers come from. Where her *mother's* powers came from.

"Looks like you won," Yumi says, tapping a bottle of water against her opposite hand.

"Did I?"

"On points, I mean," Yumi says. "You had more points over the tournament, so they're giving you first place. You're the national champion. Congratulations."

Danielle shrugs. That was never the point, and they both know it. "Only because you conceded."

"It was either that or call Muramasa in front of all those people. But that was your goal, wasn't it?"

Danielle doesn't answer that. Would that have served her goal? Isolating her? Making her desperate for allies? She isn't even sure anymore. There are so many moves and countermoves, it feels like circles. And just now, none of that really matters.

"I, uh," Yumi says. "I brought you something to drink."

Danielle sighs. "Is it whiskey?"

"I'm eighteen." Yumi extends the cold bottle of water. "Wait, how old are *you?*"

"Never mind." Silently, Danielle takes the bottle and presses it against her neck, where she felt the touch of that fiery blade of vengeance. It feels really good against her sweaty skin. She sighs, relieved, then gestures to the bench opposite. One last invitation.

"That's ok," Yumi says. "I just came to say goodbye."

"That's all?"

"Yeah."

"Ok then." Danielle's too exhausted to argue.

Yumi makes it three steps away before she pauses and looks back.

Danielle looks up, not surprised.

"I wanted to thank you, too," Yumi says.

114

That is a bit of a surprise. Danielle narrows her eyes. "For what?"

"Teaching me." Yumi's red eyes flash. "About me."

"How's that?"

Yumi smiles. "We should do this again sometime," she says. "I wrote my number on the water."

"Yeah?" Danielle pulls the bottle away from her neck and inspects the number written in sharpie. "Shit. You did." She looks up at Yumi. "I must have done something right."

"You were honest with me," Yumi says. "I hope we can be friends."

"Hmm."

Rainbow-haired Lisa arrives, and her smile fades a little when she sees Danielle sitting there. No surprise. That girl is much sharper than Yumi seems to think she is, and she does not like Danielle—not one bit.

Lisa looks warily to Yumi and holds out a tentative hand. "You ready to go, bae?"

With a faint smile, Danielle salutes Yumi with the bottle.

Yumi nods. "Yeah," she says, taking Lisa's hand. "Let's go."

As they leave, Danielle's smile turns to a grin.

Maybe she hasn't failed after all.

ABOUT THE AUTHOR

Erik Scott de Bie is a speculative fiction writer whose favored genres include fantasy, sci-fi, horror, and superheroes, and especially pieces that mix all of the above. He is also a known quantity in the gaming industry, being the author and/or editor of a number of major releases for *Dungeons & Dragons*, *Iron Kingdoms*, the Cthulhu Mythos, and others. His most recent novel series is The World of Ruin, a post-apocalyptic fantasy like *Game of Thrones* meets *Fallout*, and he is currently writing in a new gaming tie-in setting for Archvillain Games. He lives in Seattle with his wife and their menagerie of pets. Find him online at https://erikscottdebie.com/.

www.ingramcontent.com/pod-product-compliance
Lightning Source LLC
Chambersburg PA
CBHW060756120626
46557CB00009B/1073